LIVING DEATH RACE
BEAUTY & THE BRAINS

John Everson

LIVING DEATH RACE:
BEAUTY & THE BRAINS

©2024 by John Everson

ISBN: 9798332605512

Cover, layout and interior
K. Trap Jones

www.theevilcookie.com

I

Zombie Cock Fight

《《—》》

The chick was Mean. Mean with a B—spell that B I T C H. The rules said that you could only enter the Cock Fight ring with your clothes—no knives, hammers, guns or other obvious weapons. This was a fist and claw matchup, and it seemed somewhat ludicrous to pit a 110-pound kid against a 200-pound Neanderthal. But, as the announcer had crowed at the start of the match, "Looks can be *watch-your-balls* deceiving!"

Tony chewed a mouthful of popcorn and both smiled and cringed as the girl kicked a stiletto through one guy's eye. Before the guy had even hit the ground pawing at his ruined face, she'd whipped off her belt and after swinging it around three times, allowed the heavy steel buckle—which just happened to have a porcupine pattern of nails attached—to slam into the temple of the other guy who'd come at her when the first one dropped. The nails raked an instant flesh-puncture pattern across the guy's cheek, but that was just a distraction while she slipped off her other stiletto. She used the shoe to more precisely hammer the 2nd attacker in the ear and nose before she leapt at him with both feet, connecting in the belly and grinning as they both fell to the ground. She was younger and quicker to recover; she used her belt to pin his head to the floor as she stomped her remaining heel into his eyes and nose repeatedly.

The guy never even had a *chance* to bite her. Good thing, too, because his teeth looked yellow as a toddler's wading pool and his nails were black as the stuff at the bottom. The other man staggered back to his feet behind her, but "Beauty" was ready. She gave the corpse at her feet a last kick that cracked the broken head audibly from the spine, and turned to deliver a similar aerial stomp on her revived attacker.

This time she wasn't so elegant. Tony chomped his popcorn and watched as the man caught her ankle and instead of connecting with his bloodied face again, he saw Beauty fall on her tight little ass and cry out in anger more than pain. She was back on her feet 3.5 seconds later and when the zombie's hand pawed at her waist, she grabbed it by the wrist, dropped back to her knees, and in a flash that most of the audience couldn't follow (yet cheered for anyway) had the flesh-hungry hulk lying on the ground with a broken back.

Then she stomped a silver high heel spike through his eye.

She stood there, shoe inside the zombie's brain for several seconds as the crowd screamed like a cyclone in the basement room. The roar was deafening, and Mira "Beauty" Linn smiled at conquering yet another beast. Then she pulled her foot (accompanied by a slight suction sound) from the dead man's head and walked off the stage to collect her prize. She had places to go and mechanicals to buy.

Tony set his popcorn under the creaking theater seat and quickly made his way out of the school basement. But unlike the rest of the stream of Zombie Cock Fight gamblers, who quickly put as much distance between themselves and the illegal arena as possible, he didn't leave the premises. Tony slipped around the back of the long, three-story brick building, and hunched down behind a dumpster that hadn't been emptied in months. "School's Out... for EVER!" Tony heard Alice Cooper singing prophetically in his head. That was the only place Alice would be singing anymore, since Tony guessed if the rock singer was using his mouth these days at all, it was only to suck down brains. There were not many strongholds left that the walking dead hadn't eaten their way into and out of. He guessed Alice, like most of the world, was lost in the Dead Zone.

He crouched in the back of the abandoned school for a good 15 minutes before his patience was rewarded. Finally, a back metal door swung open and a small figure in red sneakers, jeans and an old grey t-shirt walked out and down the concrete stairs. If Tony hadn't paid such close attention to her in the ring, he would never have connected the high-heeled fashion plate killer with this ragamuffin street kid. But it was the same girl. He knew it as soon as he watched her walk. She moved with a rhythm that was unmistakable to an eye that paid attention.

Tony knew rhythm. He knew dangerous rhythm. That was Beauty exiting the steel door at the back of the abandoned school. And there were no beasts around but him.

He didn't intend to meet the wrong end of her heel, as so many had, in that dirty ring set up in the old school gym. So he followed her at a very safe distance as she moved down the back alley, slipped through a broken board in an old fence, and then walked along the sidewalk of an eerily quiet neighborhood. He really hung back when she ducked through a broken piece of wooden fencing, turned down a dead-end abandoned street on the other side, and pulled a steel rod from the back of her pants which she then inserted into the sewer lid at the end of the street.

Tony watched from the side of a house as the girl slipped down the hole and disappeared beneath the street. Just as her head went below ground, he darted across and leaned down to peer into the hole. He was just in time—he saw her shoe disappear out of sight, which told him which direction to head. He counted to 20, and then carefully slipped down the rusted metal ladder himself.

Tony hung his head down as low as he could and saw a ripple of motion from down the long dark sewer pipe. He moved in that direction as soon as his feet touched the ground. Two minutes later, he was crouched over at the edge of an L in the 4-foot drainage pipe. He could see Beauty slipping through a giant crosshatched grate at the end of the pipe, daylight gleaming in painfully bright from beyond.

He didn't wait very long before following.

Mira Linn took a deep breath as she stepped through the grate and out into the wasteland beyond the Millbrae Barricade. South San Francisco had been cut in half after the zombies walked, and Millbrae had offered a good route on which to build "the wall." They'd locked *in* the city but in the process, they'd locked *out* a lot of things. One of those things, was what Mira ran to now.

A 1972 Mustang.

Her baby. Well... her adopted baby.

Mira had trained for her matches in the Zombie Cock Fight by finding her way outside of the San Francisco safe zone to fight zombies in their own element. She'd killed hundreds of the slouching corpses out here and she'd continue to do so for as long as she could. It kept her sharp. And got rid of the godforsaken zombie motherfuckers. She hated the hulking creatures and wanted nothing more than to help each and every one of them lay back down in the graves they should never have stood up from.

If she had to plant a heel between their eyes to help them do that, she had no problem with that. If she had to take the undead out one brain at a time... well, she was OK with that.

But while she'd been practicing the peaceful art of death-giving outside of the safety of the city barricade, she'd discovered the candy apple Mustang smashed into the steel pole on Herron Street, and she'd kind of fallen in love. Her dad was a mechanic, and she'd worked in his shop since she was 5. It hadn't taken her too long to pry the machine away from the pole, dispose of the partial corpse that remained inside with its head eaten off, and begin work on rebuilding its broken engine and bent frame. She'd moved the car, once she could, into a fence-enclosed lot so that she could work without worrying too much that a zombie was going to take a bite out of her calf when she was half under the car.

So, she was alert. But the zombies didn't come around here too much since she'd destroyed most of the indigenous population with her feet. And those that did, couldn't figure out the lock she put on the fence—at least not before she heard them rattling around on her cage. She generally dispatched those without too much difficulty.

That's why she was surprised when she felt something grab her ankle and yank her out from beneath the body of the now nearly perfect Pony.

"Nice ride," a heavy voice said.

Mira had just enough time to register the swarthy complexion and deepset eyes of the guy before his fist connected with her face. As the stars registered and she slipped into fog, she had just enough time to think, "shit, this guy's alive!"

II

"Beauty" Meets "The Brains"

«« — »»

Beauty woke up pissed.

Tony had expected that. Nobody really comes to with a smile after being decked in the face.

That's why Tony had tied her wrists to the fence. Then he'd sat back on the hood of the Mustang just a couple feet away from her limp body and waited for her to wake up. It hadn't taken too long.

Mira realized her predicament right away when she first tried to punch him, and then aimed to plant her heel in the center of the asshole's ball sack.

Neither move worked. The fence rattled a lot, but that was all that happened. She hated the smarmy grin on his square face. It made his lips plump up and she longed to smash them.

Mira wasn't stupid. She didn't waste her energy struggling and ripping up her wrists and ankles on her bindings trying to escape. There would be time for retaliation. First, she had to find out what was going on here.

"What do you want?" she asked through thin lips. She watched as the slits of his dark brown eyes rounded and grew.

"I want to drive in the Living Death Race," her captor said. He crossed tree-trunk thick arms across a barrel chest and flashed a row of shark-white but crooked teeth at her.

"And I should care about this... why?" she asked.

"I need a navigator," he pronounced, slowly unclenching his arms and pushing himself off the Mustang. He stepped away from the vehicle and walked around it slowly, trailing one heavy finger across the metal. When he completed the circle and stood in front of the car, he looked up at Mira, and creased a fast grin before speaking.

"And I think I need this car," he pronounced.

For a few seconds, Mira forgot her self-control and thrashed against the fence.

Tony leaned back against the car and raised an eyebrow as she struggled. When she saw the wicked grin on his face widening, she stopped pulling against the metal and hissed a single word:

"What?"

Tony shrugged and nodded his head towards the west.

"They can chew you out of those, if you want," he suggested.

She followed his gaze and saw two dark figures stumbling along the road from the airport. They were headed in her direction. Drawn, no doubt, by the sounds of her struggle.

"Bastard," she hissed.

Tony shrugged. "You do whatcha gotta do."

She looked past his shoulder and saw the figures growing closer. From somewhere not too far away, a faint cry of hunger shivered in the air.

"What do you want?" she said.

"Navigator," Tony said. "Mustang."

He shrugged. "It's really simple."

"What do I get?"

"Your life," he answered with a slow grin. "And 25 percent of the prize."

"50 percent," she answered.

Tony looked over his shoulder and raised one dark eyebrow. "I can drive the car without a navigator," he said. Then he held up a chain between his fingers and added, "And I already found where you keep the key."

Mira's eyes widened as she shifted against the fence so that she could feel her right breast move against the bra. It was a personal question... and her answer was quickly apparent. There was no key tucked in her bra anymore. She pictured the Neanderthal feeling her up with his meaty hands while she was out for the count, and the image made her face burn.

"Bastard!" she yelled.

Tony shrugged and jerked a thumb at the shambling bodies with teeth that were now just seconds away from the fence. The familiar groan/growl of undead hunger filled the air as the two creatures moved steadily closer.

"It's my car," she said. "I built it."

Tony shrugged. "Well, I'd love to have you on my team," he said. "If you survive."

He turned his head to watch the zombies stagger around the side of the fence.

"Fine," Mira said. "You win, you fuckin' bastard. Let me out."

Tony pulled a knife from his jeans front pocket and slid it up through her bindings as the zombies groaned and shambled just inches away. He kicked the fence as he cut Mira's bindings, scaring the eaters off momentarily. And then she was free and falling forward from the fence and into his arms. Her feet and hands tingled bad with pins and needles, and Tony took advantage of that to clasp her close, enjoying the crush of her breasts against his chest.

"Why me?" Mira asked, planting a fist on his chest and pushing none-too-gently backwards.

"I saw you at the Cock Fight. You know how to kill them," Tony said simply.

She nodded. "Yeah, that I do."

He kicked the fence and a thin cry went up from the grey-fleshed body that had been reaching with one decayed arm through the metal.

"So, let's take some out!" he said.

"What makes you think we can survive the race, let alone win it?" she asked. "The Death Race is a suicide mission. Most of the drivers don't come back."

"That's because they don't have a hot piece of deadly ass like you riding shotgun."

Mira socked a fist into his gut. Tony flinched, but also smiled. "You'll have to do better than that, sweetheart," he said. With one hand he managed to grab both of her wrists and drew them together in an unbreakable grasp. Working with weights for most of his 19 years of life gave Tony an undeniable pure-strength advantage.

"Let me tell you about the way this is going to go down..."

III

Betting Against a Death Horse

《《—》》

"**5**0 to one!" Tony yelled in the cab of the 1972 Mustang. "What the fuck kinda odds are those? Who is screwing who?"

"I'm sure it's because Macklin-Mortis has a sexier navigator," Mira said dryly. "Maybe you should trade up."

"You wish." Tony laughed. He knew how angry Mira was with him for pirating her car. But he also knew she wasn't going to back out of this. Her car could run this gambit, but it was his connections that had gotten them into the race. That, and the unfortunate run-in that San Francisco's previous sixth spot driver, Roadkill Roland, had had with a zombie toddler who just happened to have unobtrusively burrowed into a 12-point buck's belly before he put his knife to it. Roadkill Roland had thought he'd nailed himself a tasty bit of wild venison that day. He had absolutely not expected a blackened little dead hand to reach out of that deer's gut to yank the knife away from him. And he definitely hadn't expected the tiny yellow teeth that a second later had embedded themselves in his throat and chewed and chewed until his life emptied in a crimson waterfall.

Roadkill Roland had become roadkill himself that day, thereby opening a slot in the Living Death Race that Tony—self-dubbed "The Brains"—had muscled his way into with a little help from Uncle Bobby. As he continuously pointed out, it was good to have family from the Old Country.

Mira, touted as "Beauty" to the masses, would take the winning pot, if 25 percent came her way. How could she not? All she really wanted to do with her life was soup up cars and kill zombies. She was a driver's wet dream navigator.

Certainly, she was his. Not that he could get his hands near her. Tony exaggerated a yawn and stretched out an arm that briefly touched the bare caramel of Mira's biceps before he was deftly deflected.

"Next time, I break whatever piece of you touches me," she warned.

Tony grinned and enjoyed a glimpse down the dark shadow of her cleavage. She didn't have a lot, but he liked the silky looking skin that he saw.

"Let's not start out on the wrong foot," he said. "I want to win this race."

"I'm not here to lose," Mira agreed. "So, you focus on your driving."

"You got it," Tony promised. "It's nearly showtime."

Ahead of them on the 101, they could see the crowds lined up all along the outside lanes of the Golden Gate. Since the Bay Bridge had been blown up to stop the hippie Oakland zombies from crossing over, the Golden Gate was the only other connection to the mainland once you went north of the Milbrae barricade. The race would start here at exactly 11 a.m. Pacific time. The giant electrified gates would open for a short 30-second window, and the San Francisco drivers would begin at the same time as those leaving Las Vegas and New York. The 18 cars in the race would all pass through the same cities but would likely never cross paths once the race had begun. At least, that was the theory. They all had to make the circuit from their city through the other two hub cities and ultimately, arrive back at their starting point. They could take whatever route they wanted, so long as they passed through the hub cities.

Tony pulled up behind the first four cars to stop alongside Jerry Plotnik in his Olds Rocket, and wondered how that theory would play out this year. Plotnik grinned, but it was the grin of a dog who sees a bone. Plotnik and his son were the odds-on favorites from the San Francisco teams.

Mira rolled down her window and leaned halfway out of the car to stare into the blank eyes of the other driver. Rumor had it that he had the IQ of a squirrel.

"Stay out of our way," Mira said with a completely false grin.

Plotnik grinned back. "Gog," he said. Around them, the crowd screamed out the traditional chant of the Death Race in growing volume, over and over: "Take out the Dead, Take out the Dead!"

Ahead of them, just in front of the giant 20-foot metal gates, two figures stood together, bent forward. A man and a woman cloaked only in a sheet of white. Something shifted and writhed, hidden beneath the sheet at their feet. They were the Living Flag.

From overhead, the race announcer began to speak. "Start your engines and sharpen your blades, in just 40 seconds the Living Death Race 2044 will begin, here in the last bastion of the living on the left coast..."

"You checked the oil and everything this morning, right?" Tony asked as they waited for the flag to fall.

"My car's ready for this race," Mira snapped. "You just worry about driving it."

And then a single roar went up from the crowd as the gates in the middle of the Golden Gate Bridge creaked open. The man and woman of the Living Flag extended an arm on either side, each clenching a long silver blade. As they did, the sheet of white moved to reveal the trussed figures of two struggling zombies. Then they brought those blades down as one on the necks of the dead and raised the severed heads in the air triumphant. The white sheet was suddenly colored black and red, but then with the raising of the heads, it slipped to the ground to reveal the nude bodies of the Human Flag. The zombie heads splattered them in old blood, but the drivers didn't wait to watch it drip down the blonde man's tanned chest or the woman's bare pubes. The two were meant to serve as the symbol of raw human fertility, the representation of the living surviving the dead. The crowd would enjoy them completing the ritual of public procreation on the stained sheet in a few moments, but the raising of the severed heads marked the official start of the race.

"Nice tits," Tony said, looking at the Human Flag as the tires next to them already were peeling out.

"Hit it!" Mira screamed, and the Mustang leapt abruptly past the Human Flag, just as its members dropped the heads and turned to each other to embrace. The crowd quickly closed ranks in a circle around the Human Flag as the cars left the bridge, attention easily diverted from the escaping race cars to the beautiful naked couple completing the ritual of procreation on the bloody sheet.

"Nice dick," a woman in the crowd said loudly, admiring the entry of the man into his nubile partner. Or who knows, maybe the vocal admirer was a guy... Some things in San Francisco hadn't changed since the Death.

IV

To Vegas on Wings of Steel

«« — »»

Announcer Bill: And they're off! New York, Las Vegas and San Francisco all opened their barricades temporarily to let the drivers get on the road. And quickly pulled them shut immediately afterwards to keep the zombies out.

Announcer Karen: We have a race, Bill! The ninth Living Death Race has begun. Punkboy and the Rat took an early, instant lead—they found a teenage zombie sitting on the side of the road less than a mile from the start of the race and with a quick swerve they turned him into road pizza immediately.

Announcer Bill: I hope they didn't get any zombie stuck in their radiator because that's going to reek.

Announcer Karen: You're right there. It's a hot one today! The Vegas teams are going to have a helluva a first leg because it is hellishly warm out in the desert today, with temps hitting 115. That's going to play havoc with engines which is not what anyone wants on a road full of zombies...

The Mustang shot off the Golden Gate and up the 101, through a hillside tunnel and out the other side like a bullet. Wrecked cars littered the roadside. The first Living Death Race in 2036 had found the route almost impassable, but over time, the roads had been cleared at least to accommodate a single lane.

"I hope you've found us a good route," Tony said. "Cuz I don't wanna spend the next week looking at that asshole's bumper."

Ahead of them Plotnik punched his brakes and made a sharp turn to avoid a crumpled Ford.

"I have a plan," she grinned. Her mouth opened to voice it, but her words trailed off as she stared out the side window. "It's beautiful," she mouthed, staring at the distant skyline of the City by the Bay.

Tony shrugged. "It's OK. My uncle Bobby says Sicily makes it look like a squatter's dump."

"I've never been outside the city," Mira said. "Not like this."

"Well, I'm gonna show you the whole country, baby," Tony grinned, a ray of hope dawning in his gut. Or really... below his gut. This was the first time in the past month that he'd ever seen any emotion warmer than disdain from his deadly navigator. Maybe getting her on the road would actually mean *getting her* on the road.

"Eyes on the asphalt, Brains," Mira yelled.

Tony yanked the wheel to the right and just missed driving over an abandoned wheel in the center of the road. The broken pickup truck it had rolled off of was smashed against the steel of a light pole. Mira swore as they passed a litter of bones. Some of them had been ground to dust, probably from the wheels of past racers.

"50-1 odds against us they said," Mira reminded. "Do you know why?"

"They don't know shit," he said.

"We've got shit odds because we're kids. Because you bribed your way into the race. Because you have no driving history. They figure we'll wash out in the first 100 miles." Mira crossed her arms and stared at him hard, the brown of her eyes turned black. "Every second on this road is a chance for you to prove them right. Or wrong. So, you watch the road. Always. You take a look at me, and I punch you, how's that? You watch the road and I'll watch the map."

"Open the wings," he demanded, cutting her off.

"Huh?" Mira began.

"The wings!"

Mira leaned forward and cranked the wheel in front of her. To prepare for the race, she and Tony had bored a hole through the dashboard to install the car's second wheel, and it had almost killed her to defile the Mustang that way. But this modification was one of the most important ones they'd made to the car. As Mira twisted the wheel round and round, twin metal rods raised and extended outward from either side of the front wheel wells. As the rods extended, they fanned open into what looked like a set of silver wings. But they weren't meant to help the Mustang fly.

Tony swung his wheel in counterpoint to Mira's and the car bucked and shimmied as he guided them down a ramp. The Mustang shuddered slightly as those wings connected with the three figures who had been walking slowly along the roadside. Tony's collection of Oriental fighting blades, carefully affixed to the extending metal rod frame, sliced through the bodies at 45 mph. The broken head of one rolled up the red hood of the Mustang and slapped for just a second against the lower end of the windshield in front of Mira's face. She caught a glimpse of grey skin and an empty, shriveled eye socket before the head continued its roll up and over the car, leaving a trail of black blood in its wake.

"Deathasus Rides!" Tony yelled, and punched the gas to wheel the car around. They shot up the ramp again and continued south down 380 as Mira wheeled the wings closed again. They'd cause too much drag if left out for the whole ride, but she was proud of her little modification to this muscle car. With more than a hundred blades all interlocked and pointed forward on the frame like reverse feathers, they were ready to take out any flesh in front of them.

It was the flesh *next* to her that Mira worried about.

"First blood!" Tony said.

His right hand slapped repeatedly against the wheel.

If he was a dog, he'd be a tail-wagger, she thought.

"Old blood," Mira corrected. "We do not leave the route to pick up just three points."

"We scored," he insisted.

"We need to score *big*, not small," she said. "You just got us three points. Big deal."

"Every kill's a kill."

"Some aren't worth the cost of the gas you'll burn to go get them," she argued. "And anyway, we need to bring us back some Living Dead."

"Well, we're not picking them up on the way out. I'm not riding with things flopping around in the back seat for the next week."

"No," she agreed. "But we need to hit us some zombie kids. They're worth more points. We're going to shoot down I-5 for a few hours, but then instead of going all the way to Los Angeles, we're going to go off the interstate. I think we'll have some opportunities tonight."

They rode in silence for awhile, as Tony threaded his way through a string of broken cars, and broken bones.

California in August was hot as you moved inland. California in August in the cab of a Mustang that had been driving for hours was a sweatshop. Each time they pulled over for five minutes to pee and stretch, Tony and Mira lost another article of clothing. Tony was driving in a pair of shorts and sandals, with his shirt stretched across the driver's seat to absorb the sweat of his back. Mira'd started out in jeans and a fleece by the Bay this morning, but now she was down to nothing but a loose cotton pair of grey San

Francisco shorts and a hot pink tanktop. She didn't wear a bra, and Tony kept sneaking glances, as the sweat plastered the thin cotton to her small but pronounced breasts. He could see the dark of her nipples plainly now in the late afternoon sun.

Her fist slugged him in the shoulder. "Eyes on the road," she said. "Turn right at the next street."

"That looks off the way," he said, rubbing his arm.

"Note the sign." She pointed at the bent, rusted *School Zone* notice. "We're just gonna check if it's time for recess."

"Nice call!" Tony said as they rounded the corner of the next suburban street and the view opened on a long park area. It was covered in weeds, but the constant shambling movement of the dozens of small figures ahead must have kept them beaten down as good as a lawnmower.

Mira began to crank the wheel to open the wings, as Tony aimed the gleaming teeth of the Deathasus at two zombie children playing catch in the field. Well, trying to play catch. There wasn't a lot of catching going on. One corpse would pick up the ball and shakily lob it at the other who would stumble forward. Usually, the ball bounced off the other's chest, if it reached him at all. But he'd pick it up off the ground with grey-green fingers and repeat the process with similar lack of success.

Tony laughed as the decayed faces of the broken ballplayers looked up while the car drew closer. "You're outta there," he said as the Mustang slammed into them, severing the throwing arm of one, and cutting cleanly through the torso of the next. The ball rolled away, blackened with old blood. "Game over!"

The Mustang roared and pinwheeled around the playground, mowing down the slow-moving zombie kids before most even noticed that there was an intruder on the playground.

"Swingset," Mira called out, and Tony wheeled around to gun the car straight at the swings. Three blackened children were sitting there on the black rubber seats at the end of rusted chains. They barely caused the swings to move with their low muscle reflexes... instead, they appeared to be just shifting back and forth little by little in the slight wind, waiting. Eerie.

Tony ended their years of waiting with the slice of twin wings.

"School's out!" he cried. His laugh seemed to grow more unstable with every kill.

"Sick," Mira said. "But worthwhile."

Tony considered the open field, now filled with the twitching bodies of broken zombie kids.

"How much?"

"17 kills, all under 12. Total of 51 points because you got a combo bonus. All on camera," she said and patted the small camera monitor that was wired to the car's external cams.

"It's a start," he agreed. "I don't feel so good though."

"You get used to it," she said quietly. "They're already dead, remember that."

V

Dangerous Oasis

« « — » »

Announcer Karen: We've got sad news to report Bill, and the race is just hours old. Team Russian Roulette barely got two hours out of Vegas when their Dodge Challenger overheated. They made the mistake of limping off the highway to find supplies and instead found...

Announcer Bill: Zombies?

Announcer Karen: A mob of them. And hot zombies are hungry zombies, Bill.

Announcer Bill: Sounds like Russian Roulette picked the wrong chamber. Or maybe I should say placed their last bet.

Announcer Karen: They have cashed out forever.

The first leg was easy. And boring.

They had diverted off I-5 near Fresno to add some easy zombie kills to their tally early, but after Bakersfield, the road quickly grew barren as they moved toward the Mojave desert. There was not much to see in the last four hours before their first checkpoint but wasteland. Live people would have been hard to find in the best of times there.

Dead people didn't walk here.

They had blown past Plotnik and the other San Francisco drivers quickly and since there was no assigned "route" to get to their first checkpoint in Las Vegas, eventually, they didn't even see the other cars in their rearview mirror. Nobody appeared to follow them in their Fresno detour. Which made sense. The drivers all tried to split off on alternate routes, eager to find fresh enclaves of zombies to boost their scores early. Everyone wanted their own road to mine.

Vegas glimmered like a constellation in the desert and Tony's foot dipped closer and closer to the floor.

"Don't need a navigator for this road," he grinned. "It's like my Uncle Bobby from Sicily used to say, "Use 'em and lose 'em cuz all you need is right in front of you."

"Uncle Bobby was a twit," Mira said.

"He was a wise man," Tony argued. "In the end, all you've got is you."

"In that case," Mira said, "You're fuckin' broke."

"Smart girl, huh? I won't be broke when we win this race."

"Oh, it's *we* now, is it?"

Tony flashed her a crooked grin. "We're a team, aren't we? And I can picture you tonight, right there beneath me, working as a team..."

Two seconds later Tony was rubbing his jaw.

"Drive," Mira said softly. "And try to stay straight. The city is dead ahead."

The gates of Las Vegas opened to them with a flurry of flashing lights and cheers. Reporters were in their faces as soon as they stepped out of the car, prodding them with microphones and leading questions.

"Mr. Brains, rumor has it that you bribed your way into the race," one haughty blonde said to Tony. "Do you really think you can compete with the *real* racers?"

Tony answered with words not fit for public broadcast, not exactly supporting his nickname.

"Beauty - a lot of people think it's really cute that you used to kickbox zombies," a greasy man addressed Mira. "But the Death Race is a whole new level. How do you think a young girl can win here?"

Mira smiled without showing teeth. In a blur, she punched the reporter in the gut and as he bent over in surprise, kicked him with one sharp snap in the balls.

"Like this," she said simply.

The reporters backed off after that.

Tony slipped into the soft sheets of the bed with a quiet moan. The day had gone smoothly, but that was the most driving he'd ever done in his life. Since the cities were walled up, the only time anyone got out from behind shelter to race the highways was in the Death Race. There was no way to prepare for this. You either had the steel in your bones to make it cross country and back, or you died. There was no training. This was all chutzpah.

Tony was counting on his pure physicality to pull him through. He'd hung out at the gym since he was 12, and the next few days were going to tap into all of the reserves of strength he'd built up over the past seven years.

He opened his mouth to yawn and something cool touched his lips. His eyes shot open and just above him, leaning over the bed, was a woman. Not just a woman... a fuckin' *smokin' hot* woman. Her eyes were Eastern European, her nose thin and delicate. Her lips were full and pressed together in a teasing heart. But it was her breasts that Tony couldn't take his eyes off. They seemed to defy gravity, cones of perfect creamy flesh that stood proudly out from her petite frame, wide brown nipples erect and tantalizing in the night air. His eyes had barely registered the belly button ring and the tattoo of a monster race car on her groin before she was slipping into the sheets next to him. Her skin was creamy and warm against his own. Her lips were even warmer. In the back of his mind, Tony was high-fiving himself and laughing "yes, this is what it means to drive the Death Race!"

And then it got better.

Another warm feminine body suddenly slipped into the bed and sandwiched him from the other side. She brought with her the smell of jasmine, and her hair trailed like black silk over him as she leaned down and ran an almond-skinned hand across his chest.

"I am Passion and this is Rose," the new girl whispered. "We can be yours for the night."

"We will do anything you want," the first girl, Rose, whispered as she traced his earlobe with a warm, wet tongue.

Passion slipped her body over his and rubbed the silken nubs of her chest on him, slipping all the way down his body until her lips were glancing across his balls. As she hovered there, pressing him first one way and then the other, she whispered with hot breath against his cock. "We just ask one small price."

Mira set the hotel room alarm clock for four hours, and then pulled the windup clock from her overnight bag and set it too. The rules said they had to shut down the car completely two hours a night, but let's be honest—there was no way anyone was going to survive on two hours of sleep a night for over a week. Tony and Mira had agreed that four was a good start, and if necessary, they'd add another hour as the days went on.

She slid into the sheets and was asleep almost instantly... but something woke her halfway through the short night. Her eyes snapped open in the dark, and she strained her ears to listen. Her senses were sharp; she'd grown up listening for creaks on the floorboards and footsteps in the hall. They'd alerted her to hide, or be molested.

Slowly she peeled back the sheets and reached to the floor to recover her t-shirt. She slipped it on and after making sure nobody was in her room, she eased the door open to the hall.

Mira and Tony were in a two-bedroom suite, and she stepped into their shared foyer and listened for a moment at his doorway. There was sound coming from within. She listened, ear cocked to the door, and heard someone moan loudly from inside.

Mira tried the doorknob, and it opened easily. She let herself in.

On the bed, a bleached blonde with torpedoes for tits was bouncing up and down on top of Tony's waist. She straddled his hips, grinding her own against him with short, fast, fluid jabs. She let out lamblike bleats of pleasure with each downstroke, and rubbed her palms across her belly, guiding their rhythm. Meanwhile, a dark-haired girl faced the blonde. She had a snake tattoo curling up around her naked brown waist, and the sweat on her small but shapely breasts glittered in the faint light that streamed into the room from the windows. She matched the blonde's motions, shoving Tony's tongue inside her as she shoved her own into the lips of Torpedo Tits.

Smothered between her thighs, Tony let out faint groans of appreciation.

"Get the hell off of my *Driver*!" Mira yelled, stalking into the room. She planted two hands on the blonde's chest and pushed, sending her awkwardly off balance and to the foot of the bed. She connected an open palm with a sharp slap to the ass of the surprised Oriental, who released Tony's mouth and rolled off the bed to the floor.

"What the hell is going on here?" she demanded of Tony, whose cock still stood comically tall, as he wiped his lips with the back of his hand before reaching into his mouth with a finger to tease out a hair.

"I think it's obvious, damn it. Get the fuck outta here and let us fuck!"

Mira ignored him and addressed the whores who stood together across the room. "I give you both to the count of three and then my foot's going to be on your necks. And I promise, it won't be a Kama Sutra move."

The two reached down to grab whatever clothing they'd arrived in and darted from the room in seconds. But before they left, the blonde turned at the door, one magnificent breast popping back into the room to taunt Tony's still raging libido. "Remember," she said. "We have a deal."

Mira pressed two hands on his shoulders and demanded, "What deal? Who were those women?"

"If we win, I signed them in for a cut," Tony said. "And they were worth it. What the fuck did you have to interrupt for? Goddamn it, I haven't gotten laid like that in..." his voice dropped. "Ever."

"You want to win that money, you gotta drive like a goddamn devil," Mira said. "And you're not going to do that if you don't use every minute of downtime getting some sleep. We've only got two hours left til we clear out of here, and now you're going to be shit when you wake up."

Tony reached up to grab her by the waist. With an easy hoist he lifted all of her 110 pounds off the floor and deposited her next to him on the bed. Her t-shirt rode up as he did it, and he saw that she wore nothing beneath. He slipped his hands up her ribs to cup those bare breasts momentarily in his hands.

"Then you better play the full role of navigator and guide me in," he said, slipping has hands around her back to pull her against him.

She tried not to connect hard enough to injure him for life, but he doubled over pretty dramatically as Mira slid from the bed unrestrained. She suspected his hard-on was no longer raging. And might not be for awhile.

"What'd you do that for?" he gasped, while rocking on the bed in pain.

"Touch me again and I'll break them," she promised. "Get some sleep. We ride in two hours."

VI

A Mountain Pass

«« — »»

Announcer Karen: Most of the drivers have now left their first checkpoints and are on the road again with their thirst for victory growing as deep as their thirst for sleep.

Announcer Bill: It's true, Karen. They get a luxury suite to rest in at the checkpoints, but most of them don't stay in those comfy quarters for more than the minimum four hours. They want to get back on the road to get ahead in the standings as fast as possible.

Announcer Karen: I have to say, it's been a hoot watching Team Bury-Them from New York on the road so far, Bill. They have really gone above and beyond when it comes to putting zombies down.

Announcer Jim: That's true. They have been relentless, and currently lead the field with 78 zombies killed in just the first day of the race...

Beauty and the Brains ran into trouble before they hit Denver. The route was easy since there were only a couple highways cross country for much of the route through the west, and those had been cleared of debris thanks to previous races. That also meant there wasn't a lot of opportunity to add to their kill list. The miles passed slow and quiet; zombies didn't wander where there was no meat. And most of the wastelands between Vegas and Chicago were empty of anything but broken asphalt and wind. And a rusted road sign.

The sign said Newcastle—3 miles.

"We need to refuel," Tony said. "Shall we see if we can find some old gas instead of using our own backup tank?

Mira shrugged. "Why not? Maybe we can get a couple easy points; I wouldn't think a lot of drivers have cutoff out here in the past. There could still be some walkers."

They pulled off the ramp with the bent and rusting Newcastle sign and wove through the weeds into the broken town. Tony pulled under the broken awning of a Sinclair station and killed the engine. "Now is the test," he said. "Can we get the pump working after all these years?"

He stopped the car at the pump and inserted the pump nozzle into the tank. Then he flipped the start lever and held his breath as he pressed the trigger on the gas nozzle.

Nothing happened.

"I really don't want to waste our own gas reserve if we can get some here," he said. "I'll be right back."

Tony walked towards the old station office and turned the old silver knob. The metal moved, but the door was stuck fast. Who knew how long since it had been opened? He kicked it with the knob turned, and it squealed open with a rush of mildewed air. Dust puffed off the floor and countertops near the cash register. The residue of decay hung in the air like an old halo.

He walked in and searched below the register for an On switch. Finding one didn't mean it would *work*... but it would be a start.

"There!" he said, finding a small metal lever with his finger. Hopefully it opened the floodgates from the tank to the pumps. He would still need to find the manual crank to push the fuel to the pump since there had likely been no electricity here to power the system in years.

The click echoed in the small space.

But then there was an answering click. Only it wasn't metallic. It was the sound of a heel hitting the floor.

It came again.

Tony stepped back from the register and held his breath. *Click.*

He moved towards the door, but he didn't get far enough, fast enough. A door in the wall of the station creaked open. A girl with dark wavy hair, shadowed eyes and a thin nose stepped inside.

"Hey," Tony said... but she didn't answer. She only kept walking. Her left side seemed to drag a little when she stepped, and so her foot made an uneven sound as she crossed the floor.

"Hey," Tony said again. "Can I give you a ride somewhere?"

She didn't answer, but instead, continued walking towards him. He could see her face was pale to the point of being blue... her eyes had a sheen of white over the pupils that made him wonder if she saw him at all.

But the whites of her eyes weren't what Tony was looking at. It was the white of her t-shirt... and the swell that moved and shifted under it as she walked.

"Helloooo," he said softy, as she stepped through the door. And then he said "Hello" again, less appreciatively when she kept coming.

When her face was just a foot or so from his, he put his palms on her shoulders.

"Whoa," he said. "We don't know each other that well. Though I'd like to. What's your name?"

She moaned a low tone that sounded vaguely like "Guh-uhn" and kept shuffling closer... lifting her arms to grab at his shoulders.

"Maybe I'll just call you Gwen," Tony said, sidestepping her hands. But I'm not dancing with a zombie." He reached out his hands to cup her shoulders, gently keeping her from moving any closer. His touch gradually moved lower and the girl didn't protest. Perhaps she didn't even feel it.

"I'm just passing through," he said. "In the Living Death Race… I just need to get some gas," Tony said. "I didn't think anyone was at this station anymore, but if you wouldn't mind…"

She didn't say anything.

"I could just give you some cash…"

She still didn't say anything, and Tony moved his hands up the bare skin of her sides.

He loved the feel of the soft skin beneath his hands. It was when her teeth bared in his direction that he realized that he may have made a tactical misdirection.

She didn't flinch when he held up a hand to stop her from looking at him as food.

"What's your name?" he asked.

"Uhhhggghhh," she answered. Her teeth opened and searched for his neck. Tony pushed her backwards with a hand. "Let's take this slow," he suggested. She only surged forward, looking for a quick fix… on his vein.

He grabbed her shoulders and restrained her hunger.

"No."

And when she growled and surged forward to attack, he grinned.

One thing Tony had, was strength. And nobody moved into his space without permission.

He easily grabbed the girl by the arms and dragged her forward, right to the place he wanted her in.

But with a quick switch of his arm he stopped her teeth from moving forward to latch onto his neck.

Child's play.

"Uh-uh," he said. "Now I have a few other ideas."

After securing her arms and teeth with a couple of elastic rubber tiebands hanging from the gas station walls,

he demonstrated those ideas to her in the back office she'd
been hiding in.

VII

A Mountain Pass II

«« — »»

"**Y**ou fucked a *zombie*?!!"

If Tony hadn't still been busy pushing his business inside of a dead girl, he would have seen exactly how red Mira's normally dark complexion had turned. Instead, he just moaned and grinned as he reached his climax inside Gwen. The zombie girl didn't make much sound at all; but having her arms tied to the wall and her back bent the wrong way over a short table probably didn't make the experience all that comfortable for her. If she could feel anything at all. Given no choice in the matter, she complied.

"You take what you can get," Tony huffed as he continued his last thrusts. "That's what Uncle Bobby would have said."

"Fuck Uncle Bobby, you half-witted neanderthal. You have the gall to call yourself 'Brains'? Clearly you do not have any! Do you not understand how stupid this is? Your dick is inside a fuckin' zombie! Tonight, you may be turning into one of them now..."

"No worries," Tony said, and pulled away from Gwen, whose midriff stayed prone, unmoving on the table as he retreated. Tony peeled a milky bit of rubber off his still half-erect penis and let it slip with a splat to the floor. "My motto is, when you fuck with the dead, use a death shroud!"

Mira rolled her eyes. "Jesus."

"Jealous?" he grinned, putting hands on hips and swiveling so that she could see his cock shake, lolling half-hard.

"Hardly." Mira turned and walked away. As she left, she called back, "We were here to get gas, remember?"

Tony grinned and reached up to cup the zombie's round right breast. "I'm filled up," he whispered. "How 'bout you?"

Then he bent down to retrieve his pants and shirt, before he tied the zombie up to take her out to the car. Every live zombie brought back was worth 20 points. And he figured this one was truly a bonus. She was points at the end of the race... and fun for the nights in between.

When he got dressed, Tony found a switch near the fusebox at the back of the room and threw it. Something in the other room hummed, and he smiled. Backup generator still worked! He pulled Gwen up from the table and trussed her so that her teeth could not accidentally find contact with his or Mira's skin. Then he marched her out of the abandoned station and into the back of the Mustang. She moaned a bit as he forced her into the back seat, but the black rubber in her mouth kept her from making too much noise. She shifted and flipped and growled for a few minutes in the constrained space behind the Mustang's bucket seats, but eventually she settled down while Tony got the old rusty pump to creak into motion again. The generator was still doing its duty, as he'd hoped, and after a few minutes, the Mustang and the extra fuel tank tucked in the trunk were both full of fuel.

"Let's kill some Dead," Tony laughed, as he slipped into the driver's seat once more.

Beside him, Mira didn't say a word.

Tony turned the key and smiled as the car rumbled to life. Maybe silence was a blessing.

From behind his back, however, came a low, insistent groan. When he looked in the rearview mirror, Tony saw the cloudy eyes of Gwen open wide, as she shifted back and forth across the back seat, trying to wrestle free of her new bindings. Then her face peered up fast and close to the mirror, as she threw her torso against the back of his seat again and again, jolting him against the wheel.

Something told him it was going to be a long ride.

VII

Dangerous Liaison

«« — »»

*A*nnouncer Karen: We are now more than two days into the race and things are starting to heat up.

Announcer Bill: That they are, Karen. We've got a wildfire raging in the hills of California, and the temperatures in the Badlands have reached 108 over the past 24 hours. To make things worse, there's a hurricane hitting the Florida coast, and the entire stretch from New York to Chicago is either flooding or sweleringly humid.

Announcer Karen: That wasn't exactly what I meant, but you're right, it's a Living Death Race on all levels. I have to say, I'm glad I'm not in any of those cars.

Announcer Bill: The heat hasn't slowed these drivers down. Pussy Crush and Poison Pete from New York are the early favorites, with 97 points in just 50 hours of driving.

Announcer Karen: They have taken a lot of sidetrips off the highway to get that score, which is slowing them down, but if they keep up this pace, they could be the last drivers to finish and still win the race.

Announcer Bill: That's something all the drivers need to keep in mind at this point. It's not simply about getting back to your starting point ahead of everyone else, though that's worth a lot of points. But it's the combination of finish position and zombie kills that ultimately solidifies the victor.

"I need to pee," Tony said. His forehead was beaded with perspiration. The car felt hotter than hell; he cringed at the steady stream of sweat that slid from his shoulders down the crack of his ass. It was amazing that he had anything in his bladder to complain about given the amount he was sweating. It was hell outside as well as in. The brown fields around them seemed to shimmer in and out of focus with the unrelenting heat. "Are you ready yet? I've been waiting a half hour and it ain't gonna wait much longer."

They'd agreed to only stop when both of them needed to release; they couldn't afford to be stopping every hour because their bladders weren't on the same schedule.

"Sure," Mira agreed. "And things look pretty empty around here. I haven't seen anything moving since Des Moines."

Tony nodded and began to slow down as he weaved around the abandoned cars. Driving I-80 was like a marathon obstacle course; the cars weren't thick, but they popped up every mile or two, often inconveniently in the middle of the lane they were driving. Mira had agreed that it was smart to not stop within sight of an abandoned car because zombies could be slumbering in the back seats just waiting for the scent of fresh blood to wake.

When he'd put the last car behind them by a mile or two and couldn't see another one yet on the horizon, Tony braked fully and stopped.

Zombie Gwen moaned behind them. The thing sounded anxious.

"Pretty sure you don't have to go," he said as he pushed the driver's side door open. He walked around the hood of the car, stretching his legs as he moved to the side of the road to unzip and let loose. He didn't look for anything to hide behind; there was no one around but Mira and Gwen to see his action. And he didn't care if they saw his junk let loose in the midday sun.

Mira, on the other hand, exited the car and walked to the opposite side of the road, stepping into the tall grass there until she was hidden from the road. The last thing she was going to do was drop her shorts and squat in full view of Tony.

He grinned as he looked over his shoulder to see her disappear into the weeds. Uppity bitch for a junkyard fighter. He'd nail her by the time this trip was through. He could feel it. She couldn't say no forever. In the meantime, he had Gwen. He just wished she'd move with him when he did the deed instead of shifting against him like an earthquake. The thought of that brought a thickening to the tool he held in his hand and he tried to think of something besides Gwen's perfect—if faintly blue—tits beneath him. He needed to pee in the grass, not in his face.

He focused instead on the fact that they needed to find gas soon. The fill-up they'd done when he found the zombie had nearly been exhausted and the Mustang's gas needle had been inching lower and lower as they traversed the endless plains of the highway. They were probably going to need to stop at another of the forgotten small towns touted by the bent and rusting green highway signs before they reached the next major city.

He could hear the hum of the Mustang's engine in his head, growing desperate and whining for gas. You needed to feed the beast. While he'd chosen a car with an engine that wouldn't quit, it admittedly wasn't as efficient as some of the other engines driving this race. For every plus there's a minus, he thought, as he finished releasing his stream.

As he shook off, and reached down to zip, he realized that the hum of the engine wasn't just in his head.

There was someone on the road behind them. Coming in fast.

"Shit," he yelled across the road. "That's Kill Bill and the Cootch. Get back to the car NOW!"

There was no prize in the Living Death Race for killing other drivers; in fact, if you damaged another driver's car, you lost points. But... there was a loophole. If you happened to catch a driver or navigator along the road—outside of their vehicles—there was no penalty for taking them out of the race.

Permanently.

Tony dashed to the driver's door and scanned the weeds across the road for some sign of Mira. He panicked when he didn't see her at first. A glance to his left showed the souped up red 2007 Dodge Viper that Kill Bill always drove. You knew it was him from a distance because the center of the hood was bisected with a wide black stripe. The word

K

I

L

L

was stenciled down the center. The car was close enough for him to read the deadly promise of its hood and was slowing down. That could only mean one thing. Kill Bill and the Cootch intended to take out Beauty and the Brains.

"Hurry!" he called.

Mira's dark hair suddenly bobbed above the weeds and a second later, her yellow sneakers hit the gravel on the side of the road.

But it was already too late. The Viper screeched to a halt between her and the Mustang, and the driver and passenger doors flew open. Kill Bill, a thick-muscled bruiser who stood at least six foot four but had shoulders that seemed almost as wide, leapt to the ground and instantly moved in on Mira, one hand outstretched.

Instead of dashing across the broken asphalt, Mira regrouped, ready for a fight. But she quickly realized there wasn't going to be much of one. Kill Bill held a black pistol confidently in front of him as he moved, the barrel focused dead on her forehead.

Mira's instincts had long been honed in the arena to expect and react to the unexpected. They played her true here. Without a thought, she dove to the ground and rolled, just as the first shot rang out. The bullet parted weeds instead of her hair, and Mira aimed a fast jab to Kill Bill's knee before he could get off a second shot. The big man jolted, stumbling forward a step before starting to turn.

Mira knew she could take this buffoon in a fair fight, so her first rule of order was to make it one. She came up in a crouch and aimed a karate chop right at Kill Bill's wrist. The air reverberated with a shot that rang Mira's ears, but luckily careened harmlessly off the asphalt. The gun clattered to the ground as Kill Bill cried out and Mira kicked it into the ditch as she leapt to her feet.

Now she could show this numbnuts how training and speed beat beefcake every time.

The red door of the Viper shot open and the razor-sharp machete bolted onto it nearly took out Tony's gut as it did. He jumped to the side as the Cootch emerged, a mean-looking grin on her narrow weasel-like face. The tip of her electric pink mohawk clipped the top of the doorframe as she emerged, tan and half-t-shirted, bronze thighs looking very ready for action. But the action Tony would have wanted from them wasn't what she was about at this moment. Word on the street was that The Cootch was a nymphomaniac as well as a car fetishist. Kill Bill supposedly nailed her all the time on the hood of the tricked out Viper in full view of anyone who cared to watch. But right now, those muscular thighs meant pain, not pleasure. She held a hatchet in one hand and a switchblade in the other. She came out of the car swinging.

Tony didn't even try to defend himself. The flash of silver in the air was almost blinding in the mid-day summer sun and instead of trying to disarm her, he stumbled backwards away from the Mustang, and all but threw himself off the road and into the ditch. She'd have a harder time accurately slashing on uneven ground with four-foot-tall grass all around.

"San Francisco only needs one team to bring home the trophy, and that team ain't you," The Cootch said with a hissy whisper. The swish of the air as her blades whipped back and forth only accentuated her airy voice.

Tony turned and began to run through the weeds, the sharp edges of tall grass cutting at his skin as he ran. The bitch was not far behind; he could hear her breathing. Or her blades. He wasn't really sure which. And he really didn't care as long as she didn't catch him. Tony was not used to running away from a chick, but this chick looked deadly.

He tried to run in a broad circle, mindful of not getting too far away from the car, when his foot caught on something in the weeds. The ground rose up with a whoosh of green and brown blades of grass. His face suddenly kissed the hard earth with a rude slap.

But not as rude as the red hot pain that suddenly sliced across his shoulders.

The Cootch had found him right in the position she liked her men.

Prone.

Mira did a roundabout with one leg outstretched and ready to connect with the wide target range of gut that Kill Bill presented. But big Bill had other plans. He grinned and literally just... threw himself at her.

Speed and agility were a big advantage, but they had nothing on a moving wall. Just ask Wile Coyote. Kill Bill gave an audible "ooof" as her foot punched that fat pad he called a belly, but a moment later she was shrieking as his weight collided with her and drove her to the ground.

Hard.

She felt pain flare in her left shoulder and then a deeper heat filled her chest. Mira prayed he hadn't just snapped one of her ribs as the warm, damp weight of his chest smothered her face to the ground.

Mira wasn't going to just lay there and let him crush her. Her arms and legs may have been trapped, but her mouth wasn't. You used whatever weapons you had.

She opened wide and let the soft flesh of his broad chest roll into her mouth. When she couldn't let any more of him in, she bit down as hard as she possibly could.

The effect was exactly what she was going for.

Kill Bill screamed and shoved his body off and away from her, dragging her head off the ground with him until she unclenched her jaw and let go.

Sometimes the smallest pains are the ones most effective.

She didn't ponder the result, but instead rolled fast to her right and bolted to her feet. Crushed ribs or not, she wasn't going to go down that easy.

Mira pivoted.

Kill Bill looked angry as hell, his eyes wide and his mouth open in anger at the pain from her teeth. Before he finished yelping about a little bite, Mira punched her heel into the white row of teeth he had left undefended.

Based on the throbbing of her foot, she didn't think many of those teeth were still attached to his jaw a second later. She didn't look to find out. Instead, she twisted and aimed a punch directly at his throat.

It connected.

She could feel the trachea collapse beneath her knuckles.

Kill Bill went down like a ton of bricks. That body slam he'd aimed at her was suddenly him versus the ground... this time, he was the victim. He was out.

The tortured choking sounds he made as he writhed on the asphalt barely registered with her. She looked once to make sure he was immobilized and then turned to see what "The Brains" was up to.

He didn't have any he could afford to lose.

The Cootch was going to chop his head off.

Tony knew it without any doubt. Her thighs—thighs of steel—had him pinned to the ground even though he weighed more. She held the axe above his face, poised to come down any second, severing his last thoughts on this earth from his last desires. His body wanted more but his mind couldn't seem to make it move. He laid there, understanding suddenly that it was the last second of his life.

And realizing just how much that sucked.

The Cootch grinned, her mouth a row of shiny teeth that looked more like a shark about to feed than a smile. She clenched her arms to dole out the death blow.

The Cootch looked happier than a fuckin' clam.

Until a yellow sneaker connected full force to the side of her head.

Beauty had intervened.

The Cootch twisted in the air in a way that the human head was not meant to twist, that victory grin of a moment before replaced with a grimace of *what-the-fuck-hit-me?*

Tony was just as shocked as The Cootch. He'd been saying his Hail Mary's a second ago.

"Come on, numbnuts, get on your feet. We've got a race to run."

He took Beauty's extended hand and hauled himself to his feet with a groan.

The Cootch lay on the ground, eyes wide open, the axe abandoned a few feet away. She wouldn't be needing it again. Her head was bent at an angle that said The Cootch wouldn't be finishing the Living Death Race. Not as a driver or navigator anyway. She'd soon be a zombie with incredibly bad posture.

He retrieved the axe and followed Beauty to their car. No reason to leave a good weapon to rust.

When they passed Kill Bill, also staring skyward on the ground, Tony made a mental note of just how dangerous it was to be on the wrong end of Beauty's anger.

VII

Deep Inside The Night

«« — »»

Announcer Bill: It's no surprise that New York's Pussy Crush and Poison Pete continue to hold the lead with 109 kills. They are utterly relentless.

Announcer Karen: It's true. I watched their navigator, Pussy Crush wake up from a sound sleep on the ground next to their car and snap a crawling zombie's neck between her thighs. An instant later she took off another's head with a blade that looked like something my grandad used to have on the farm back in Iowa. This girl takes no prisoners.

Announcer Bill: Yeah, you don't want to get in her way, that's for sure. Her driver is no slouch either. Poison Pete has taken out at least two dozen zombies so far in the past three days simply using his hands.

Announcer Karen: Seems like a great way to get bit and lose the race.

Announcer Bill: You'd think so, wouldn't you? But until they invent fast zombies, I think he's okay. He moves like a Cheetah.

"You have to keep driving," Mira said.

Beside her, Tony groaned. His complaint was echoed from the back seat as the zombie shifted and struggled against her bindings.

"I've been driving for 14 hours and I'm tired," he said.

"You're tired because you keep fucking instead of sleeping," Mira answered. "I'd take the wheel if I could, but we'd be disqualified."

"I wish I'd been the navigator," Tony grumbled.

"I thought Uncle Bobby said it's better to lead than to read?"

"Uncle Bobby sucked."

"I'm glad you finally admitted it. Now keep your foot to the floor."

The car lurched forward in the darkness as he pressed his heel down harder. "We need to find someplace to stop," he complained. "I can't keep doing this for much longer without a couple hours of sleep."

"Well," Mira said, "Now that you've filled the back seat with cargo, I don't know *where* you're going to sleep."

"At this point, two hours sitting straight up in my chair without my hands on the wheel would be enough."

"I hope so," Mira said. "Because that's your only option."

"Well... then we're pulling over for awhile," Tony said. "And this looks like as good a place as any."

The headlights cut through the dark like yellow pillars... all around them the black locked them in.

"This is it," Tony announced, and stopped dead in the middle of the empty road.

Behind him, Gwen growled and complained as the engine powered down.

"I'm going to sleep."

Tony rolled over in the bucket seat and eased it back as far as it would go.

"Wake me when the dawn comes."

Mira pulled out her mechanical travel clock and twisted a knob on the back. "You've got two hours."

It felt like his eyelids closed over grains of sand. Tony wanted nothing more than to be out of this horrible seat.

His ass was numb and sweaty, and his lower back could not find a comfortable position no matter how he shifted. Beside him, Mira drew her legs up and curled into a ball, head resting between the edge of the bucket seat and the window. Behind him, Gwen began to let out a quiet but high-pitched keening. It went on and on, and Tony shifted and swore. Finally, he turned and grabbed the zombie by her calf. He shook her until those milky blue eyes fastened on his own, and the noise stopped.

Stopped just long enough for him to settle back in his seat and close his roadburned eyes so that the sting began to ease.

And then the keening began again. Tony shook the dead girl up again.

"Keep it up and I'll cut off your tongue," Tony growled.

"I don't think she needs a tongue to make that sound," Mira's voice mumbled.

Gwen quieted again for five minutes, and then the birdlike wail began again.

"That's it," Tony said, and threw open the driver's side door. "I may have to sleep in this car, but she *doesn't* have to."

"What are you going to do?" Mira asked, rolling over to observe with unmasked amusement. "Tie her up outside like the family dog? No trees around here."

"Better than that," Tony said. He pushed the seat forward and dragged Gwen out of the back seat. He pulled her to the front of the car, and then lifted her whole body and sat her bare ass down on the hood of the Mustang. Leaving her hands bound, he untied her feet, and then one by one fastened them to stems of the Deathasus wings. Then he forced her to lie back and used the elastic ties he'd taken from the gas station to bind her wrists to the driver's and passenger's mirrors.

At last, he slipped back off the hood of the Mustang and looked at his captured prize spread-eagled on the hood of Deathasus. The down of her sex looked soft and inviting in the blue-white light of the summer moon. Her legs glowed in the light; the moon stripped away all of her death marks. Even her eyes looked sexy as Gwen threw her head back and forth on the hood, struggling to loosen her bindings.

Tony grinned and watched her writhe on the hood. She wasn't going anywhere. But he enjoyed watching her tits shift and roll as she tried. Around one of them, some medieval kind of script was tattooed and he leaned closer to read it: Grigori 3 it said. He didn't know what that meant, but he felt himself responding to the sight of this trapped, half-naked woman, and under his breath, he said "What the hell. It will help me sleep." He unfastened his belt and kicked his jeans to the ground. Then he climbed onto the hood of the car and slid his erection between the long-dead, bluish-purple lips of her sex.

"Oh yeah!" Tony moaned. He grabbed the ripped and moth-eaten material of her t-shirt and pulled once. The cotton ripped away easily, revealing the round flesh of her breasts. The undersides were dark with the bruises of old death, but the nipples still puckered invitingly (if a bit greyish) beneath the stars to Tony, and he suckled one as he thrust inside her.

Beneath him, Gwen's voice keened higher and higher. He took the sound as a prod to orgasm, and moved faster, a piston on her hips. *This wasn't going to take much time away from sleep at all,* he thought.

"That's what I'm talking about," he cried as the zombie's whole body tremored and banged against the hood of the car. She was like an epileptic in seizure beneath him and while they certainly weren't meant to, this time, her spastic motions only helped him along.

"Damn," Tony said a moment later, and eased himself off the girl and the car.

Gwen still shook and whined, rolling her head from side to side and pushing her hips off the car and back again. Tony laughed, thinking that her motion looked like she was still trying to fuck the ghost of him above her.

"We're done baby. Maybe we'll go again tomorrow."

Tony pulled on his pants and crawled back in the car.

"I didn't want to see that," Mira said quietly. "I *really* didn't want to see that."

"Next time, close your eyes," Tony said. And then he closed his, and despite the still audible keening of the zombie, he was asleep in seconds.

The car rocked.

Tony felt it, but he was deep in a dream that involved six brunettes, a stick of butter and one extra long zucchini. He was pretty sure he knew what was going to happen to the zucchini based on how the girls were sharing the stick of butter. What worried him was the car battery and the two long cables extending from it. Each one had a small clamp at the end, and one of the girls had just attached one of the clamps to the thin skin of one of Tony's testicles, before she was called back by one of the other busty brunettes for a butter douche.

Tony had a bad feeling she'd be coming back in a moment to attach the other clamp, completing the circuit, now that her crotch glistened with an oily sheen. And for some reason, he couldn't seem to move. He suspected that when she attached the second clamp, he'd move.

A lot.

The brunette came back. She had really sweet brown eyes and a thin, delicate nose. Tony could have lost himself in her chest and pale but pretty lips. She looked sweet and wholesome and kind. And she smiled sweetly as she lifted the other battery lead and moved it between his legs until he lost sight of her hand.

And then his whole world shook.

Something crashed nearby.

One of the girls screamed.

Only… he realized the screamer wasn't one of the brunettes who were now writhing lasciviously nearby passing the zucchini. It was Beauty.

"Wake up Tony," Mira yelled. "Now!"

Tony opened his eyes and at first couldn't understand what he saw. The body of Gwen still glowed with its deathly reflection of the moon on the hood. But beyond her, things were moving in the night. In the driver's side window, a shadow loomed and twisted. And then two blackened hands slammed against the window.

Tony jumped. "What the fuck!"

"Your girlfriend's little lullaby apparently called them," Mira said. "Start the car."

Tony turned the key and the Mustang roared to life. The headlights suddenly illuminated a mob of at least two dozen of the dead shambling ahead of the car, never mind the ones that already surrounded it. Next to him, Mira cranked the handle and unfurled the Deathasus wings from the sides of the Mustang. When she couldn't turn any longer, she said two words.

"Punch it."

Tony did. The car leapt forward, tremoring as its deadly "wings" and the knives on its front bumper collided with rotting zombie flesh. Legs fell to the left as torsos toppled right. The car shook and lurched but kept going. Tony went to the end of the crowd, and then slammed a foot on the break and whipped the wheel around, turning a 180 on the loose gravel that covered the road and aiming the car back in the direction they'd come from so that he could go pick off the rest of the mob.

This was an *old* group of zombies, he thought, as their sunken grey faces hung there, frozen for just seconds in his headlights, just before the car slammed into them and the lipless rictus of decayed and yellowed teeth opened to scream in ... anger? Pain? Hunger? What did the dead feel when they were killed again? As their bellies were opened to release the blackened, rotted husks of their old organs and their thighs were sliced off like trees in a logging operation?

Their clothes hung in the most desiccated rags and their hair, those that had any left, hung long and twisted and gnarled from sickly white scalps.

These were the oldest dead, surely. The original zombies. Tony felt good putting these to rest. Like his old friend Piccirilli once said, it was long past time for them to just *fucking lie down already.*

When he crisscrossed their path three times and could find no more moving targets, Tony hit the windshield wipers and the glass spray. Black blood washed down the sides of the front window like thick mud. As the glass cleared, he could see in front of him that Gwen's beautiful chest and belly were covered in the same black rain. But otherwise, his zombie doll appeared no worse for the slaughter. Her head shifted back and forth as she struggled to free herself from the bonds. He caught a glimpse of the milky orbs of her eyes as she looked up and back at him. He could have sworn he saw hatred there.

Could zombies hate? It hurt him to think they could. As rough and bestial as he'd treated her, Tony didn't want anyone to hate him. Uncle Bobby said that hate was for the lost. A winner never hated anyone... he always found something in everyone that he could use.

Mira pulled him from his egocentric thoughts.

"37," she said simply. "And the cameras were all working fine. That puts us in contention now. If I'm counting right, our score should be closing in on 100 at the moment."

"Sweet!" Tony said.

VIII

New York State of Mind

«« — »»

Announcer Bill: The Living Death Race doesn't simply spell death for zombies.

Announcer Karen: No, Bill, that's the truth. Every year, more than half of the contestants who begin this race never return. We have already lost one team from each city. We saw Las Vegas team Russian Roulette barely get out of the starting gate this year, and then on their first stop to refuel, New York team Punkboy and the Rat, who were the kill leaders at the very start, were surprised by a literal wall of zombies. The things were all just sleeping in a line inside the gas station. The team walked inside and the undead things all just... woke up.

Announcer Bill: But zombies aren't the only deadly obstacles on the road cross-country and back.

Announcer Karen: No, that's for sure. The drivers themselves can be as dangerous as the dead.

Announcer Bill: Yes, and San Francisco's Kill Bill and the Cootch severely underestimated the kick power of their rival San Francisco team Beauty and the Brains. They thought they'd caught the pair with their pants down... and in fact, they did. The two were, um, watering the grass on the side of the road when Kill Bill and the Cootch decided to pull over and get rid of some of their competition. But Beauty singlehandedly—or should I say, singlefootedly— sent both of them to join the zombies.

Announcer Karen: Just proving once again who the deadliest of the species really is, Bill. Girl Power for the win.

Announcer Bill: She has certainly raised the standings of Beauty & the Brains. They started this race as the long-odd underdogs and Vegas now puts them in the middle of the pack.

Announcer Karen: There are still a lot of miles to go, Bill. Pussy Crush and Poison Pete currently have the lead and Snakegirl and Siouxsie are right behind. Those New York teams are fast and efficient. And over the past few hours, Team Master and Servant from Las Vegas have whipped their way into third place. Beauty will need every bit of that energy she showed against Kill Bill and the Cootch to finish this race. A little help from the Brains wouldn't hurt either...

"If I have to watch his pale white ass pretend it's the goddamn moon one more time, I'm going to kick it until there's no white left on it."

Mira sat in the navigator's seat of the Mustang. It was night, but the faint light of the moon made Tony's ass all too clear in the window. It looked like an oil derrick, rising up and down and up again above the hood of the car. Mira had been forced to stare at the object it was mining for the past couple days, as they drove through the barren fields of the Midwest and began to angle north, towards New York City. They'd plowed through a few dozen Undead, but really, it had been a hot, horrible, silent trip. The naked zombie tied to the hood of the car had been the main source of background noise for the ride. That and Tony's endless stories about Uncle Bobby. If she heard one more story about that crooked Italian mobster, she'd throw up. The only thing that had stopped her so far was that she knew if she puked in the car, she was going to be the one to clean it before it baked its way into the carpet forever. Lord knows the male chauvinist pig driving her car wouldn't lift a finger. He'd just tell another story about how Uncle Bobby had thrown up once...

The zombie let out a high-pitched squeal, answering Tony's guttural moans. And then he was getting back in the car, face flushed, smile a mile wide.

"I just gotta say, she is the best..."

Mira stopped him with a word.

"Don't."

"But, I just have never..."

"Don't care."

"She makes me feel..."

"Don't wanna know."

"But..."

"You've got three hours to rest both of your heads and then I'm going to start yelling."

Tony rolled over in the bucket seat and smirked.

"I know you want it," he said.

He didn't get an answer.

Mira watched Tony as he slept. It wasn't because she admired him and *wanted* to watch the drool stream from his slack jaw to pool onto the driver's seat.

It was because she hated him.

Mira had never felt so strongly in all her life. She might be more inclined to hug a poor, shambling zombie than she was to put her arms around Tony, the sad, selfish son of a bitch. Mira wanted to kick the shit out of the zombie fastened to her car's hood—that filth should not be lying on her car. But she had more feeling for the dead girl right now than she did for Tony.

She only knew one thing. She had to end this fuckin' shit. And the black marks she'd noticed creeping down

Tony's neck told her that the time was drawing imminently, inescapably closer.

Her thoughts were broken by a long drawn-out snore, as Tony slipped deeper into sleep.

Bastard. Now he was going to keep her awake.

Mira's heel itched. It ached to bury itself in that smug jaw lying next to her.

Soon, she promised. *Soon.*

"So, what's the route today, Beauty?" Tony asked when Mira punched him awake in the dark before dawn.

"Don't call me that," was all she said. "Because I'll be damned if I'm ever calling you Brains. Just drive."

"Where to?" he asked, yawning.

"New York City," Mira answered. "We should be almost to the checkpoint."

"Think our odds have risen?" he asked. The Mustang revved and growled to reach its standard pace as Tony pressed his foot to the floor.

"We're halfway there," Mira said. "We can't have gotten any worse in the gambler's statistics."

He shrugged. "Depends what you're gambling on."

The day seemed to go on forever. Mira could feel the heat of the eight cylinders bleeding through the floorboards and into the balls of her bare feet as the Mustang veered around abandoned cars, broken glass and broken bones all along the highway leading towards the Big Apple.

Deathasus plowed through a half dozen more shamblers on the way into New York... but aside from a few black marks on the ever-visible breasts of Gwen, they were none the worse for wear as they pulled across the bridge and into the checkpoint for the Death Race.

"17 to 1," someone said, as they passed through the gated entry to Manhattan.

"1 is all that we're after," Mira said, with a falsely pleasant, fuck-you smile.

As soon as they left the car in its guarded, assigned spot in the checkpoint garage, they were besieged by a crowd of reporters.

"Snakegirl and Siouxsie pulled in just ahead of you," a reporter announced. "They've already scored 109 kills, and a lot of double points. They're the popular favorites halfway through the race. Do you think you can possibly beat them?"

Beauty stuck her tongue out in disgust. "Trust me, I know just how to handle snakes."

"Beauty, we've heard that your driver has a special thing for the Undead," a particularly vapid reporter said, shoving her way forward. Her eyes were abrasively large and blue and she sported a particularly vapid smile.

Mira pushed past her. "I've heard that you like to have your tits chewed by the dead," she answered sweetly. "I could help arrange that. Our girl is hungry."

The reporters backed off.

They were down to 15 teams, so their odds had increased.

Mira intended to make sure they continued to soar. After Tony went to bed, she followed him into the hotel room. She hadn't locked the connecting door between their suites.

"That's what I'm talking about," Tony said when he felt her slip beneath the covers with him.

"Don't get your hopes up," Mira said. "One word about Uncle Bobby or a roll-over with hands intent to grope... And you're done. I'm here for one thing, and one thing only. To make sure no other tit-head gets in your face and stops you from focusing on the race. We only have a couple hours to sleep... so just fuckin' do it, ok?

It was hell to have Mira lying next to him... but Tony couldn't complain.

Well... he *could*. He wanted to fuck the shit out of her, but he knew if he tried there'd be very little left of him the next morning.

Tony rolled over and thought about Gwen. *She* didn't turn him away.

He thought about the dark discolorations on the undersides of her breasts and the grunting toothy responses he got when he told her how he felt.

Words were beyond them now. But in his head, he found himself whispering them anyway.

"I want you. I need you."

His consciousness recognized the ridiculousness of someone getting sweet on a zombie. She was just a corpse, after all. He knew he'd kill her again in the end... but for now...

Mira listened as Tony's breathing evened out to a low snore. Every now and then, the bed shook, as his body trembled from some inner fear or pain.

Mira looked at the black hairs that curled down the nape of his neck and disappeared beneath the sheets with his shoulders. The black marks on his neck that had been getting darker over the last couple days of the drive; she didn't like to think of the meaning of that but she had to be ready for what that meant she'd have to do. He shivered, silently next to her, and Mira shook her head.

She knew she'd have to kill him in the end... but for now...

IX

Sweet Bones, Chicago

«« — »»

Announcer Karen: There is really nothing like the Living Death Race. I just can't take my eyes off the race car cams. It has been a non-stop bloodbath out there. This has been an exciting day, hasn't it Bill?

Announcer Bill: It has. And a deadly one. The latest Team to learn what the Death part of Living Death Race means was Jerry Plotkin & Son, a team from San Francisco. They were on the road back from New York and got caught in a torrential storm in the Cuyahoga Valley south of Cleveland. Plotkin tried to swerve around an abandoned car in the middle of the highway and instead skidded right off the pavement and down an embankment.

Announcer Karen: I will never forget that last footage from their rear bumper cam, as he and his son were trying to push the car out of the ruts it made, and a grey hand reached around Plotkin's face and covered his mouth.

Announcer Bill: That was a shocker! And a second later, those decaying black teeth bit into his neck. For a moment that camera feed literally dripped with red. Talk about a dramatic end.

Announcer Karen: They haven't made a horror movie with a more perfect moment. That footage has already gotten over 10 million views on the web. I'm sure the memorial service for Plotkin and his son—who was eaten by three other zombies a minute later—will be packed. But

I'm afraid it will be a closed casket. There wasn't much left of them for the official Living Death Race crew to recover.

Announcer Bill: The field continues to narrow. The Vegas team, Death 'n Dice also got knocked out overnight when their car was attacked by zombies while they were sleeping.

Announcer Karen: That is the danger at this point. These teams are utterly exhausted from running most of the week on catnaps to put the most miles behind them in a day. At this point, we're about three-quarters through the race and Pussy Crush and Poison Pete still lead with over 157 points now. Snakegirl and Siouxsie have dropped to third, as Master and Servant continued their push for domination.

Announcer Bill: Ha! They've managed to whip up 143 points at this point. But Beauty and the Brains have also emerged from the middle of the pack. They started this race as the underdogs and now have managed to scrape up 138 points. They are just two behind Snakegirl and Siouxsie.

"I always wondered what Chicago really looked like," Tony said quietly as the Mustang rumbled down the broken highway. He was truly exhausted. The drive from New York had been a white knuckle special. As soon as they managed to get past a squall line, they found themselves in the midst of a new storm. They drove for a couple of hours, and at one point were barely able to see more than a car length in front of them... which is extremely dangerous when the highway is littered with abandoned vehicles. It was a very slow, silent ride. Eventually, they'd been forced to leave the highway for local roads when they encountered a multi-vehicle crash that looked as if it had involved dozens of cars and trucks. They couldn't go around it, so they'd had to reverse course five miles and take an exit to drive through local roads temporarily.

All in the relentless, pounding rain.

But at last, the rain had dried up, at least for awhile. The sky roiled in grey discontent above them as they passed through a line of abandoned suburban businesses and homes. In a Chicago suburb that a sign said was Oak Forest, they passed a lonely tin man who waved a frozen welcome from the roof of a heating and air conditioning shop not far from the highway. Rust trails had driven brown trails of tears across his once-cheerful tin man face. A few miles from there, they'd gotten back on the highway and passed a wasteland of rusted car parts that seemed to stretch on forever near a grown-over canal. ABC Auto, the sign by the junkyard read. Mira thought it should have been called XYZ—not the beginning, but rather the end of the line.

Ahead of them, the silent spires of the dead cityscape of Chicago loomed ahead. While miles away still, it looked impressively close. Size mattered in architecture, as well as... other things.

An old green road sign announced that the old White Sox stadium was just ahead. "I need to make a stop," Tony announced. He took the next exit and pulled onto a road bordering the highway. The road was an obstacle course of abandoned cars, with doors left hanging open and windshields shattered.

"Where are we going?" Mira asked.

"I need a drink," Tony said, and pulled into the lot of a seedy one-story building labeled plainly and simply: LIQUOR.

"Really?" Mira asked. "You're dying from lack of sleep because you keep fuckin' a zombie; you can barely keep your eyes open and you're jerking around like an epileptic, which means you probably have caught the virus from your dead whore. And you want to pour *booze* on top of that? I'd personally like to score some cash out of this stupid race. Could we just drive, please? We've got like, three more days to go, at the least."

Tony looked at her with eyes ringed by deepset shadows and said four words. "Shut the fuck up."

He got out of the car and walked to the front, trailing one finger across Gwen's bare breast and belly before tracing the skin of her thigh until he reached her knee.

"I need a drink," he repeated to himself and walked up to the door of the abandoned liquor store. He pulled on the knob and the door didn't budge. Without a second thought, he hauled back and planted a sharp heel kick into the glass of the door.

It shattered in an explosion that was still settling when Tony crouched down, reached a hand through the hole, and opened the door from inside.

Somehow this place had survived the apocalypse relatively intact. The walls were still lined with bottles of vodka and whiskey and gin. Tony took a bottle of each and grabbed a bottle of tequila to boot.

As he stepped back through the door, he could hear Gwen's dead vocal cords keening in that high-pitched siren call that she had. Tony shrugged and opened a bottle of vodka and poured a slug into the zombie's open mouth until the sound shuddered, gargled and stopped.

"That's better," he said.

He slipped into the car and handed a bottle of Canadian Club whiskey to Mira. "Time for a party," he announced.

"We need to drive," Mira said. She wasn't sure what to make of this Tony. He'd always been unbalanced, but focused. Now...

"I need to rest," he said. "My back aches, my neck aches, my head aches. I'm tired and I just want to have a couple drinks and chill for a couple hours. I need this. I can't drive anymore for awhile."

He opened the bottle of tequila and took a slug. He closed his eyes and coughed. "Yes."

Mira shrugged and opened the bottle of whiskey. She poured back a swallow and gasped. Then she sank into the seat and pulled up her alarm. "You've got four hours," she said. "And then you gotta drive again. I don't care how fucked up you are. We're too close to fall behind now."

"Deal," Tony said. He drank another swallow. "Did you ever wonder what zombies feel?" he asked.

Mira shook her head. "They don't feel a damn thing, man. They're dead. I keep telling you that. Why do you think I killed so many of them? I was just finishing the job. They were already gone."

"Gwen can feel me," he said. "I know she can. I see how she looks at me."

"Her eyes are fucking clouded over, you asshole. She doesn't know anything except that some Neanderthal is pushing and prodding at her."

Tony beamed. "See—you admitted it... she knows that I'm there. That means she can feel."

Mira rolled her eyes. "A magnet repels another magnet... that doesn't prove it feels anything. It's just physics—it does what it does."

"She knows I'm there," Tony said, pouring back another drink. "She knows I need her." And then he announced, "I gotta piss."

He got back out of the car and walked to the edge of the parking lot to take care of business.

Mira laid her head back on the bucket seat. They were so close. And Tony was cracking. In every conceivable way. This was his junket, he'd basically kidnapped her into it... and she was going to be left with the mess to clean up at the end, she could feel it. She needed that end to have a prize attached for all she'd been through.

Mira felt the car move before she heard the noise. She opened her eyes, and saw Gwen's head shifting back and forth, as the zombie's hands slapped, trapped but frantic, against the hood of the car. The dead girl looked as if she was trying to break her bonds and launch herself from the hood of the Mustang by pure energy.

"What the fuck?" Mira whispered, and sat up straight in her seat.

That's when she saw them.

The Dead. A horde of them. Walking.

Moving around both corners of the old liquor store.

"Tony!" Mira screamed, opening the door. He turned at the sound, his penis still visibly streaming in the twilight. The sight didn't excite Mira. "They're coming," she yelled.

At that, Tony's head ripped around, and he saw the grey-skinned dead filing out from the dark corridor between the buildings. They'd been waiting for someone to come. Anyone.

Fresh flesh. And there he was, alone and unarmed, just begging to be eaten.

Mira pulled a long iron rod from the back seat and got out of the car.

"Come on, man!" she yelled. "Now!"

Tony fumbled his zipper and turned to head back to the car... but three zombies already blocked his path. He feinted right but when the zombies moved to follow, he dodged left, kicking out at the closest one to put it off balance.

Ahead of him, Mira swung the tire iron like a bat. Zombie brains spilled from rotten flesh like blackened, foul yolk from old eggs. She took down the shambling carcass of an old woman who may have been 60 when she died, but now looked more like 100. While they didn't grow old in the human sense—zombie children were always children—the furrows of death deepened every year as the flesh on their undead bones struggled against itself to dissolve. The old woman's head came off easily with the force of Mira's swing, and the headless body stood still for a moment, as if unsure of what to do. Mira had already launched into a swing at a grey-faced teenager when the woman's body at last toppled over behind her.

Mira stood in the center of a growing circle of hungry dead. They tried to move forward to grab at her and bring her to the ground. But she never slowed, swinging her bar round and round, taking out one zombie after another, sometimes breaking arms and legs, but usually crushing skulls. The ground around her grew slick with stale blood. The air grew rank with the taint of rotted, old death.

Tony ran to help her but then stopped short when he saw four of the dead surround Gwen. A young zombie with ratty blond hair reached out to touch Gwen's bare leg. She stroked the skin and tried to pull the dead girl's limb towards her.

Next to her, a man in the rags of what had once been a blue t-shirt reached out to put the fat fingers of blackened hands on Gwen's unprotected breasts.

Tony's jealousy was instantly aroused. "Get away from her, you assholes," he yelled, and brought his fists up to pummel the back of the older zombie's head. The girl turned away from Gwen to reveal a face virtually stripped of flesh. Her stained teeth were unhidden by lips; those had rotted away long ago. The white of bone protruded around the white film of her eyes, and her teeth looked abnormally long and yellow without the clothing of lips. They clacked as she turned her biting attention from Gwen to Tony's arm. He felt her start to fasten on to his forearm, but before she could break the skin, he brought up one knee and caught her in the neck. She fell back, and he kicked her to the ground before returning to punch the decaying face of the older zombie again and again, until his fingers were cut and bleeding and the zombie's face no longer looked grey, but streamed with the blackened rot that had been pooled in that place where once there had been a brain.

"Fucker," Tony screamed again. "Don't *ever* touch my baby," and with a final punch the zombie fell twitching to the ground near the girl. But the other two had now moved around the car to converge on him.

Tony backed up and hopped onto the hood of the car. His back leaned against the comforting dead flesh of Gwen, and he kicked out at his new attackers, catching them in the chest and repelling them again and again. They didn't stop trying. And soon there were more than two, as the circle around Mira broke up (in many cases, literally, as she stripped them of parts). The attention of the dead mob switched from Mira (too dangerous to eat) to Tony (difficult, but clearly not as much as Mira.)

They surrounded the car now, and Tony retreated to the center, sitting between Gwen's legs so that he could pivot back and forth and protect her. In his mind, they all wanted his girl, and he would die before he let that happen.

The yellowed fingers of old women and young men and children clawed at Tony. Behind him, Gwen's voice went into that keening ululation, and he turned to look at her and saw her head swiveling back and forth, as hands grabbed at her hair and chest as well. He laid himself on top of her, sheltering her dead body with his.

"I won't let them hurt you," Tony promised and leaned down to kiss her. A second later, he screamed, and pulled back, eyes wide with surprise and blood dripping from his mouth.

Blood bloomed from his thigh and belly as two more zombies fastened on to him with their teeth. From both sides of the car the gnarled hands of the dead grabbed and pulled at his shirt until they'd gouged holes in the cotton. With a long tearing rip, it finally came apart, exposing the flesh of his back. The hunger cries of the horde rose higher as they saw the flesh, and the fresh spots of warm blood.

Mira continued to bash out zombie brains, working her way towards the car. When she cleared enough zombies to see the bloodied body of Tony, still hugging his Gwen, she shook her head in disgust. "Always thinking with the wrong head," she said to herself. Tony looked up at her in pain and confusion, his eyes unfocused. Mira was sure he'd contracted the virus from Gwen days ago. Sex with a zombie? Who would be so stupid? But now... there was no question. Tony had hours left before he turned zombie. Maybe not even that much.

"There's only one way out of this one," she yelled above the growls of the hungry dead. "Uncle Bobby would have told you to keep using a raincoat."

And then Mira brought the tire iron down on the back of Tony's head. Once, twice, five times. When his neck was ripped and broken, and the back of his head dark with purpled blood, Mira turned to the approaching dead and dropped her iron. Her arms were exhausted, but this was her arena. She'd trained for just this moment for years.

She kicked out and caught one zombie square in the nose. Old blood bloomed, and she followed that with two punches to the gut before turning to kick out fast and hard at the rotting face of another woman poised to bite. She heard the teeth clack hard against each other as her kick smashed the creature's lower jaw upwards. She turned back to the first target, who had regained his balance. With a roundhouse kick, she snapped his neck.

Mira had never been in a ring with this many zombies before. She knew she couldn't take all of them out. They were slow, but they were too many. And they were hungry.

She'd already killed two dozen of the monsters, but there were at least that many more converging on the Mustang. All she could do now was get back to the car.

She kicked again and again, shoving two child zombies back, and then she came face to face with... him.

He stood at least 6'4, and must have weighed 300 pounds. He wore only the rags of a wife-beater sleeveless t-shirt that had once been white. Once. Now it was stained yellow and brown and black. Tufts of silver hair bushed out from the neckline. He wore no pants, but the shriveled, grey lump of his penis was nearly obscured anyway by the rolls of hairy belly that ballooned out beneath the bottom of the old t-shirt. His flesh was mottled; some of it grey, some blue-black where his blood had settled and died. Long sallow streaks ran across the folds of his belly.

Mira forced herself to stop taking in the visual horror of his girth. The man made a strange sound. His eyes seemed to pop out of his head as they fastened their attention on her, and his mouth cracked into something like a smile. She knew he was only preparing to open his mouth to bite, but he looked different than the other members of this shambling horde of hunger. He looked... evil. A carcass of gluttony, come to feast on her. As if he was her true challenge. The gate between death and life.

Finally, it dawned on her what the sound was that he was making.

Deep in the zombie's barrel chest, he was laughing.

And then he rushed her.

Mira didn't think twice. She kicked.

The man was too tall. His belly met her leg before she could reach his jaw, and he bowled her over with his fat. She fell to the ground and the zombie threw itself to join her, arms outstretched to grab, teeth opened to bite.

Mira rolled and recovered fast, as his cold meaty hands clawed at her calves.

Somehow, the giant moved almost as fast as she, and was back on his feet when Mira was only a few steps closer to the car.

The zombie roared and charged, a bull in man's flesh. Mira began to run one way, and then doubled back toward the rest of the dead. She wasn't going to win this one with her feet. She had no spike heels to plant in his eyes as she usually did in the Cock Fight ring, and she couldn't even kick that high given the barricade of the dead man's enormous belly.

She swiped the crowbar from the ground and didn't slow as she wheeled around and with a vicious swing brought it up against the side of the zombie's head. The blow stopped him in his tracks, and with another angry screech, he fell forward, grabbing with both hands at her arm.

Mira felt the clammy cool hands close on her, dragging her down. If he pinned her, it was all over. She could never escape his weight.

She moved. Mira let herself start to fall with the man, but then risked everything for one fast kick. She threw herself in his direction, smashing her foot into his face as her whole body moved sideways. This time, her heel connected with his chin, and as they both landed on the ground, the force of her leg propelled them apart. His head snapped back, and she slid from his grasp.

He let out a noise that was not a laugh.

Mira rolled again and kicked at the knees of a girl with a gory gash of a nose, who had only bones left for fingers. The girl toppled, and Mira stood up and ran for the car. Her hands fumbled with the handle, as the roar of the behemoth sounded right behind her. And then it was open, and Mira slid into the driver's seat, yanking the door closed with a slam that just beat the pound of dead meaty hands on the window.

She locked the door and leaned over to unfurl the Deathasus wings.

Tony's body remained on the hood. The blood from his head had pooled and run down the long slope of the Mustang's body. Gwen craned her head, trying to get close enough to bite him, most likely.

Mira turned the key and revved the car's engine, startling a couple of the zombies trying to use Tony for lunchmeat. Then the banging began again on her window, and Mira hit the gas.

The Deathasus blades sliced off the legs of a dozen zombies before Mira skidded the car around and came back to make a second pass. Black blood rained over the car and the grey broken asphalt and Mira just kept driving in twisted circles, knocking down anything that moved. Then she stopped, lined up and smiled as she found the target she really wanted. The behemoth. The fat man had staggered to its feet again, despite her beating. Damn zombies never learned when to pack it in.

"Die motherfucker," she whispered, and punched her foot to the floor.

She drove the car straight into his distended belly. Foul chunks of something that was many years past qualifying as human splattered and coated the hood of Deathasus, and then the zombie fell out of sight, disappearing beneath the car.

Mira put the Mustang in park, and pulled out a revolver and extra ammunition from the back seat. Then she stepped out, onto the battleground.

The air stank.

Not surprisingly, since the scene was a slaughterhouse of rot. Decayed zombie legs and arms lay everywhere, some of the pieces still twitching.

There didn't appear to be any still lurking near the building, but Mira didn't intend to hang around long enough to attract newcomers. Still, to get credit for the kills in the race, she had to make sure the ones she'd mowed down were dead.

She walked around the field, aiming the gun execution style at each forehead, shooting each of the dead to death. Again.

When she'd expended 37 bullets, she returned to the car, and dragged Tony off the hood. Then she released Gwen's ties, and pulled the zombie off the car hood too. She was careful not to get near the creature's teeth, but after spending days pinned in place, the girl wasn't able to move her arms or legs very well, so re-tying her arms and legs to prevent her from getting away was easy. Then she ripped a strip of cloth from her shirt and tied a gag around the zombie's mouth. "Sorry," Mira said. "Can't have you trying to chomp my neck while we're driving. But I'm not going to make you ride on the hood, either. I don't care if you *are* already dead."

She got Gwen seated in the back of the Mustang, and then pulled a large machete-like blade from the trunk. She held it out in front of her, and hefted it, testing the balance by swinging it ever so slightly in front of her. Finally, once satisfied, she nodded, and walked over to where Tony's body lay on the ground. Then with two motions she raised the heavy blade up and brought it down, easily severing Tony's head from his body.

"I'm leaving you the brain you use," she said to his corpse, picking up the head as it rolled. "This one, I need for the judges."

Mira carried Tony's head by its hair to the car, and set it on the seat next to Gwen. Then she slipped back into the driver's seat and started the engine again.

"Alright kids," she said to the quiet back seat. "Let's hit the road."

Gwen made a faint moaning sound. Tony's head didn't say a word. There would be no more Uncle Bobby stories, Mira thought, and smiled.

She squealed the tires as she made the turn back onto the highway.

It felt really good to drive again.

X

Roadside Assistance

«« — »»

Announcer Karen: Things have taken a ghoulish turn for Team Beauty & The Brains from San Francisco.

Announcer Bill: That's right, Karen. I'm afraid Brains picked the wrong liquor store to rob.

Announcer Karen: That drink cost him his life, but his Navigator refused to let that end her hopes to finish this race with the prize.

Announcer Bill: But is she still eligible? I thought both the Driver and the Navigator needed to finish the race.

Announcer Karen: Beauty has that covered. Not only is she bringing back the head of Brains, but if she finishes, I believe she'll also get extra points for it because he's a zombie now. I think she was the beauty and *the brains of this team. As long as she and that head walk across the finish line...*

Mira woke with a start. She had pulled over not long after passing North Platte, Nebraska. The road for the past hours had been empty of zombies and her eyes were nearly fried from staring at the endless line of empty highway that cut between slowly rustling brown waves of summer scorched fields. She heard the distant repetition of her alarm and shook off the remainder of her sleep to look at the clock.

"Holy shit," she cried. She was supposed to have taken a four-hour nap. She'd been out for over seven.

"How the hell did I sleep through that?" she cried. From the back seat, Gwen answered her with a keening moan.

Mira swore again and moved to put her key in the ignition. And then realized she needed a bio break before getting back on the road. She looked out the front and back windows to make sure the road was clear of zombies before unlocking her door and stepping out to the asphalt. It was only 9 in the morning but the road already had waves of heat visible in the distance. It was gonna be another hot one.

She began to walk towards the front of the car to pee in the ditch at the side of the road, when a figure suddenly stood up from where it had been crouched behind the Mustang's hood.

A woman.

Mira knew instantly who it was from the outfit. She had black raccoon eye makeup and wore a black vinyl bra with small silver chains that draped across her bare midriff to connect to the black vinyl short shorts that barely covered the top of her pubes. Her feet were also encased in black, with heavy tightlaced boots sporting thick stomp-ready heels. Midnight black hair coiled in a braid at the back of her neck. Even with more than half of her body exposed, Mira wondered how Servant handled the heat in that getup. She had to be drenched in sweat beneath the places the vinyl hid.

A whip cracked behind her, and Mira twisted just in time to see Master, the other half of the famed BDSM duo step out from behind the rear of the car. Now she recognized the black Master & Servant hearse parked a few car lengths behind her and kicked herself for not paying attention to it before. She'd ignored it when she woke and scanned for zombies, brushing it off as just another of the thousands of abandoned vehicles she'd seen on the highway. Nope. That one hadn't been there when she'd gone to sleep.

The duo had apparently both been hiding out of view, waiting for her to wake up and unlock the door. They couldn't damage her car by the race rules. But *she* was fair game if they caught her outside a checkpoint.

"We were starting to wonder if you'd ever wake up," Servant said with a low, cigarette-rough voice that sounded femme fatale sexy. "We've been tossing pebbles on your windshield for ten minutes now."

"Thanks for the wakeup call," Mira said. "I really appreciate you stopping to check on me. But we should probably all get back on the road."

"Oh, we'll be getting back on the highway, don't you worry," Master said. He showed a wide block of teeth that suddenly seemed too large for his mouth. Cruel canines that enjoyed inflicting pain.

"But I'm afraid you've reached the end of the road," Servant finished his unspoken message.

Mira made a grab for the car door handle, but the crack of the whip hurt her ears just a split second before the sting registered like the breath of a flamethrower across her wrist.

"You know we can't let you do that," Master said. His voice was calm. Disturbingly quiet. It radiated danger. "That car is like your safeword, and I'm afraid there are no safewords allowed today."

Mira eyed the distance between her and Servant. She knew Master was too fast with the whip and would take out an eye before she reached him if she tried to go straight for him. She had no doubt that she could beat him in a fair fight, but she needed a weapon—or a shield. She needed to get the goth girl between him and her.

"I hear you lost your Brains," Servant said. A look of faint amusement tickled her eyes. "Such a shame. We're here to take your Beauty."

Mira locked eyes with Master, as she counted off in her head.

3-2-1

With a pirouette, she threw herself in the opposite direction, intending to catch Servant in that pale exposed white belly with her heel.

What she hadn't counted on was the blade in Servant's boot.

The girl kicked out one black boot as soon as Mira was in motion and the sun glinted off the wicked three inches of razor-sharp steel that emanated from the thick black toe.

Mira saw the danger but couldn't abort her kick. Instead, she tried to turn her attack into a dive. The move just barely saved her from being gutted. Instead, the blade caught her on the outside of the upper thigh. She felt the heat of the slice at the same time as her cheek met the gravel strewn pavement. She skidded awkwardly and painfully to a stop on the faded yellow stripes in the middle of the road. Her legs and shoulders burned with instant road rash. Before she could recover, a hand grabbed her hair and yanked her face up from the ground.

Servant's head blocked the blue of the sky as her dark shadowed eyes looked down at Mira. "Damn. That's gotta sting."

Rough, heavier hands suddenly yanked at her wrists and a rope began to wind tight around them, trapping her arms behind her.

"That's better," Master crooned. "Now stand up and let's see what's so *beautiful* about you."

Servant yanked her hair again and half dragged her to her feet. Mira could feel the heat from the scratches on her face spreading up her cheek. She could also feel trails of blood begin to drip down her leg from the knife wound. This was not looking good.

"Strip her," Master commanded.

A moment later, black-lacquered fingernails slid across her chest, and with a quick yank, ripped the old cotton from her neck. When the shirt didn't simply fall in half, Servant held up a pocket blade and sawed the stubborn threads until the remnants fell to the asphalt.

"That was my favorite shirt," Mira said.

Servant laughed, and then yanked Mira's running shorts down. When those dropped to her ankles, Servant slid a knife between the skin of Mira's thigh and her pink bikini underwear. With a flick, she released the tight cotton from one leg, and then did the same to the other side. Servant leaned in with a sinister grin, close enough to kiss. "Hope you didn't like the panties," she taunted, as the ruined cotton joined her shorts and t-shirt on the ground.

Master let out a long catcall as Mira stood before him naked, but for her shoes. Her exposed skin felt the burn of the morning sun immediately.

"That's one pretty pussy right there, yes it is," he said, slowly walking around her. "Short and sweet."

Servant kept a hold of her hair, lest she try to bolt.

"I wish we had the time to do a real Master and Servant session with you," he said, stopping his demeaning walkaround appraisal at last to stand right in front of her. "We typically like to spend hours showing our slaves the bittersweet edge of pleasure and pain. Helping them find their limits. And pushing them beyond until they cry for more." He reached out and took one of her nipples between his thumb and forefinger. Then slowly he began to press his fingertips together and twist.

Somehow, Mira resisted screaming. She refused to give him the satisfaction. Her face remained stoic, expressionless, which only made Master laugh. He released the now well-bruised nipple and stepped back. "Hold her," he commanded, and on cue, Servant's long thin arms wrapped tightly around her. One hooked in front of her neck, while the other cupped and massaged her breasts. Mira tried to shrug her off, but in her ear, a soft voice whispered. "If you resist or try to make a move, those little zombie slashers in my shoes will slice the tendons behind your ankles. I will make sure you can't run. Ever."

To illustrate the point, Mira felt metal scratch lightly up and down the back of her leg, just above her shoe. At the same time, the woman's fingers slid back and forth across her breasts, feeling her up with clear desire.

"Cover her eyes, not her tits," Master demanded, and Servant instantly complied.

A moment later, the whip cracked.

Mira's whole body shook, as the leather tip hit the soft skin at the bottom of her left breast like a lightning strike. A second later, it cracked again, this time hitting her other breast dead on. This time Mira couldn't hold back the shriek.

"That a girl," Servant whispered in her ear. "Let him know you're enjoying it."

"Let me go."

"You're not going anywhere."

The whip cracked again, interrupting them. It drew an angry weal across her bare belly. And then it smacked her again, just a few inches lower.

Mira could feel the welts raising on her body. It wouldn't take many hits for the blood to start to flow.

The whip slapped again, this time across her side, and she moaned in agony. "Stop it, please stop!"

"I told you there are no safewords allowed today," Master said with a laugh. He hit her again with the whip and laughed when Mira tried to double over. Servant's arm squeezed hard across her throat and kept her upright.

"It does seem a shame to waste such a beauty without enjoying her a little first, don't you think?"

"If you say so, Master," Servant answered.

"I do," he said. "Lean back on the car and keep her close to you. I can enjoy her right there. The road's too damn hot."

Mira could at least agree with that. The heat from the asphalt rose up her legs in waves. Her entire body already felt sunburned from just a few minutes standing there nude, and her skin, where it crushed against the vinyl and flesh of Servant was swampy and wet. Her entire body was weeping, though she wasn't sure which hot drips rolling down her skin were sweat versus blood at this point. It wouldn't matter if she didn't find a way to distract her captors.

Servant pulled her backwards, and leaned against the Mustang's driver's door. She pulled Mira against her, which was... sticky. Uncomfortable. Mira could feel the swell of Servant's boobs against her shoulderblades. That wasn't so bad; it was soft, though hot. But the chains that the girl wore across her midriff dug against Mira's backbone. She realized almost immediately why Master had asked for her to be in this position though. It pulled her off center and backwards, which forced her thighs to spread. She was naked, spread and ready for him.

Master was getting himself ready to enjoy it. His hands were busy undoing his steel-studded black leather belt. And as soon as his pants dropped, he shivved down a pair of dark blue underwear to let his wang wag free. It was clearly a tool that was ready to be used. It bounced out into the blazing sunlight like a jackhammer.

Mira did not want to be the ground that that tool split.

"I'd rather train you like I did Servant," he said, shambling forward, pants around his ankles. "But I have a race to win, so, I'm afraid a touch of the lash and a splash of the splash is all I have time for. Just know that if I had the time, I would really have changed your world."

Mira snorted.

Master moved closer and closer, a look of hungry desire coloring his face. Mira didn't know why he was even interested; Servant should have been enough for any guy; the "cushion" supporting her was the perfect icing on girl cake that Tony would have called "a hot piece of ass."

But instead, Servant was content to hold another woman for him to plow.

That was fucked up.

Also... her time was running out. As soon as Master got his rocks off, Mira knew she was going to be lying on the rocks. Ready for the vultures, if there were any in this godforsaken place.

Her clock was counting down.

And the jackhammer was now positioned six inches in front of her, a black-haired burly hand gripping the base and readying it for use.

It was really now or never.

Mira drew in a breath. She had an idea of how this could go. But she had to make it go fast. And the timing was everything. If she missed... she'd never walk again. Both because her tendons would be sliced and because she'd be dead.

Master held out his jackhammer in front of him like a dousing rod. From what Mira could see, he was going to hit water pretty soon. Which was all sorts of disturbing.

Behind her, Servant's breath tickled the hair on the back of her neck. Why did the vinyl-and-chain sexpot agree to lay there as a human couch for Master to fuck another girl on?

Mira couldn't fathom it, but in the end, it didn't matter. All that mattered was that the back of her head hit the forehead of the "cushion" behind her as hard as a hammer.

1-2-3 she said in her head.

With a whiplash whack, Mira slammed her head forward and then back to connect like a sledgehammer on Servant's forehead.

Before Master could grasp what had just happened to his navigator, Mira pulled her knee up in a hard, fast jerk.

That knee was positioned to connect right beneath Master's "jackhammer."

In all likelihood, that jackhammer went limp immediately. But Mira wasn't there to observe.

Master doubled over with a completely undisciplined shriek at the same time as the soft body serving as Mira's couch slid down the hot metal of the Mustang to collapse. senseless on the ground.

Mira didn't stick around to observe the results; she threw herself clear of both of them, even as her head throbbed from the pain of connecting with Servant. But she didn't go far. She was not out of this yet, not by a long shot. Her hands remained tied. She wasn't getting far in that state. So... she couldn't go far. She had to finish this now.

Like she was trained to.

With her feet.

She pictured herself back in a zombie cockfight.

All power. No mercy.

Mira aimed a kick at Servant's long white neck. The girl was just starting to rise again from where she'd slipped to the ground against the car.

And then she was choking and gasping for breath, as she fell all the way to the asphalt this time, both hands grabbing at her throat. Her eyes bulged with shock.

A second later, Mira connected the same foot with Master's teeth.

It wasn't her favorite place to land a kick, because teeth always managed to bite. Even if unintentionally. She felt the graze of enamel across her skin but the pain was worth it.

Master slumped to the ground like a deflated balloon.

Mira aimed a second kick at his jaw and smiled grimly as she heard the snap.

She shouldn't have to worry about his whip again. But what about Servant?

The half-naked vinyl and chains freak was blinking rapidly as she tried to push herself up from the road, using the Mustang as her ladder.

Mira took the rungs out.

She aimed a kick at the girl's stomach, and as soon as it connected, she twisted, without even thinking, and aimed another kick. She was back in the ring, and in the ring, if you didn't kill the zombie, it killed you. So you kept moving.

Servant's head snapped to the side in a weird and fast way that said she was dead.

Instantly.

And just like that, Mira stood naked and victorious, the tables completely turned, in the middle of an asphalt oven, with two corpses laying beside her car.

Deathasus was ready to ride again. So long as she could get her hands free to drive it.

She realized that for a while now, there had been a low keening cry coming from inside the cab of the Mustang. It was probably 120 degrees in there by now. And Gwen was apparently not immune to the heat.

The girl was dead but still...

Mira moved to the front wheelwell and found the edge of the wings of Deathasus. They were not extended, but she could still slip the bindings of her wrists over the edge of the blades.

The first attempt to run the blade over her bindings drew blood.

"Shit," she cried.

The wings were razor sharp for a reason. She hadn't anticipated needing to use them for herself. They were supposed to sever zombie limbs, not cut rope.

A couple of painful scrapes and a minute or two later, and her bindings slid free.

When the rope fell away from her wrists, she massaged them for a moment as she stared at the two corpses laying next to her car. The eyes of Master seemed to stare at her with an angry, accusatory glare. She didn't take the bait.

"Hey, I didn't start it," she murmured.

She'd finished it though.

Mira shook her head and looked at the bleak, sunburnt landscape all around her. She was alone in a wilderness of death. Not for the first time, she asked herself what the hell she was doing out here? She should be back home in the ring. That's where she was comfortable. That's what she did well. She should not be driving a carful of the dead through Nebraska. Still... here she was. Naked on a seemingly endless road next to a car with zombies chained up in the back seat.

The keening registered again with her head, and she looked up to see the zombie's face plastered to the back window.

"I'm coming," Mira said. She didn't know if the zombie understood, but she quickly picked her clothes from the ground. She stepped into the jogging shorts and then opened the door of the Mustang.

The seat was going to suck to sit on. But there was not much she could do about it but dive in.

She slid onto the leather and let out a gasp as the heat branded her backside.

There was no time to complain or contemplate. Mira turned the key still hanging in the ignition and pulled away from the two corpses lying in the road. Maybe they would have turned into zombies and she could have killed them again, but right now, she just wanted to floor it.

She didn't even care about the points.

XI

Back to the Bridge

«« — »»

Announcer Karen: We are now entering the final hours of what has been one of the most memorable Zombie Death Races we've ever held. Everyone who remains in the race is now on their last leg home.

Announcer Bill: And we've had another team leave the race this morning.

Announcer Karen: Indeed we have. Master and Servant from Las Vegas decided to try to lure Beauty—the navigator and now also driver for San Francisco's Beauty and the Brains—out of her car so that they could reduce their odds.

Announcer Bill: But Beauty seems to have used the attack to reduce her own odds.

Announcer Karen: That's right, Bill. Naked, with her hands tied behind her back, she managed to still kill both Master and Servant. Using only her feet.

Announcer Bill: I think she chose the wrong name. She should have been called the Sole Survivor...

The drive back past the Rocky Mountains and into the desert beyond was a lot less eventful than the drive to New York had been. Every now and then, Mira talked to herself, and she grew used to the familiar answering groans of Gwen. For a few hours, it was fine. She eventually stopped and pulled on a shirt, and just past Denver found a parking lot where there were a handful of zombies wandering mindlessly around.

When she left, they were wandering no more. If the last reported scores still held, she should now be in the lead. If she could be the first or second driver to reach her home base again, the combined scores for speed and kills should bring her the prize.

But for the past few miles, her anxiety had grown.

She and Tony had banked on finding places along the route to siphon fuel and replenish their backup trunk tank. The last place she'd been able to do that had been yesterday. San Francisco was now on the horizon, but the Mustang's gas tank needle hovered just above E. All her reserves were gone.

Mira had pulled into three different towns over the past two hours, and in none had she been able to find fuel to refill her tanks.

"Fuck, fuck, fuck!" she moaned. She had come too far, gotten too close, to fail now.

Behind her, Gwen moaned too.

The toddler zombie she'd stolen from its dead mother's arms in Omaha gurgled black spittle next to Gwen with a wicked dead baby grin.

"What are we going to do kids?" Mira asked her dead passengers. "It's still a long way to walk."

Tony didn't answer; the sunken eyes of his decapitated head just stared straight ahead at the seat in front of him. The toddler was strapped in but had enjoyed tying his oily hair in braids and knots while Mira drove. He looked like a failed Medusa. Tony hadn't said much since she'd separated his head from his body. Mira was okay with that.

They were just starting to traverse the endless San Rafael bridge when Mira saw them. A band of the undead, moving slowly, but resolutely towards her. She leaned over and cranked the makeshift wheel to expand the Deathasus wings, intending to take them out as she drove across the bridge. But as the wings creaked open, the engine coughed. It wasn't a good sound.

Mira felt the car lose power beneath her foot. She stomped the gas and for a moment the Mustang bolted forward... and then the engine stalled again.

"No fucking way," she swore.

Deathasus stalled three quarters of the way across the San Rafael bridge. She still had a dozen miles to go before reaching the Door of San Francisco entry blockade at the end of the Golden Gate.

"OK, this sucks," Mira said. The zombie mob was just yards away from the car. She sighed and raised her eyebrows. "Showtime, I guess. And nobody here to see."

Mira exited the car, popped the trunk and retrieved one of Tony's machetes. She held it a moment in her hand, and then shook her head, and dropped it to the ground, replacing it instead with a tire iron. Then she picked up a roll of twine and slipped it inside her shorts. If she'd been a boy, the resulting look would have been quite impressive. As it was, it looked kind of ridiculous.

The first one was easy. Two kicks and a blow to the knees with the iron, and the zombie was down on the ground. Mira quickly pulled a knot around his wrists and left him just as the next one attacked.

The second zombie was not quite such a pushover. He looked like he'd worked in a garage just before turning. He still wore a gray shirt stained with black grease, and an old mechanic's grease rag tailed from his back jeans pocket. Mira kicked at his face, but somehow, his slow reflexes still managed to stop the kick from landing. He swung his heavy arms around and caught her in the calf, throwing her off balance. Mira stumbled back, just as a woman came up, arms outstretched and voice hungry with the call of flesh.

The greasemonkey came at her and Mira twisted and slammed against the zombie woman, using her body as a wall to rebound against. Then she was kicking again, once at the mechanic, and then flipping around to plant a foot in the gut of the woman. Now there was a third zombie, a small girl, who circled the three of them, looking for a way in to take a bite of the tantalizing live flesh moving so close. Mira's fresh flesh...

Mira knocked out the young zombie's front teeth and then punched at the greasemonkey as he charged. She caught him in the cheek. The resulting crack was strangely satisfying. He lost his balance and fell to the ground, legs twitching. Mira rubbed her knuckles on her jeans. They felt slimy after the touch of the dead man. But she had no time to consider that, as the woman grabbed at her shirt. Mira pulled the twine out from beneath her belt and instead of backing away from the woman, she used the twine to attack.

She dropped her tire iron and with two hands held out a length of thin rope and ran at the zombie, catching her across the breasts. Narrowly avoiding the creature's teeth, she slipped behind the woman and deftly knotted the twine, pinning the woman's arms. The child had gotten up so she kicked it to the ground again, and caught the man in the side of the head with her two fists clenched as one. As he stumbled, she grabbed a length of twine and then ran at him, catching and wrapping him just as she had the woman. Then she kicked him in the back of the knees, toppling him. She tied a fast knot, punching out at the zombie girl as she finished it.

Something grabbed her by the hair. Mira screamed. How had one gotten past her guard? She tried to throw her body away from the attacker, but the grip held her fast. She turned just enough to see an older zombie—a man. It had brambles caught in its long silver hair which trailed over narrow bent shoulders; its eyes were empty, blackened pits.

She realized it had found her by hearing or smell, not sight. Its eyes had been gone a long time.

Good, she thought. She could use that. But before she could figure out how, the dead converged. Five of them surrounded her, blackened fingers outstretched, grasping to claw at her flesh. Mira couldn't protect her back, so she decided to "disappear." She let her knees go limp and dropped to the ground, which yanked her hair free from the old blind dead man. Lying on her back, she spun around, kicking out at each zombie in turn. She heard a kneecap pop, and one of her attackers went down.

Mira kicked another in the groin, and as it fell backwards she saw a black stain spread across its crotch. Ouch.

She brought down two more before retrieving the tire iron and leaping back to her feet. The blind zombie was the first to zero in on her again, but Mira darted around behind him, and before he could zero in again on her scent, she'd smashed his head with a fast bat of iron.

After that, the fight was finished quickly.

Mira doled out a second death to eight of the zombies, and tied up six more, including the little girl. She linked all of their bindings together, carefully avoiding their claws and teeth, ultimately forming chain gang of zombies. And then inspiration struck. Mira ran a loop of twine around the waist of a big Mexican man and cinched it. Then she darted back and looped the other end of the rope around the car's front bumper.

She stood back and nodded. There was now a line of six zombies all struggling to move forward and reach her.

Mira saw a couple of the other zombies that she'd clobbered beginning to fidget and try to rise from the roadside, so she grabbed the twine, secured their hands, and lured them over near the car before attaching their bodies to the bumper as well.

She put Gwen and the zombie toddler at the front of the line, and was just about to begin walking when she exclaimed, "Oops, almost forgot."

Mira ran to the car and put it in neutral. Then she reached into the back seat. When she returned to the front of the line, she held something in her hand.

Her fingers were clenched in Tony's hair. Beneath her knuckles, his mouth hung open slackly, a thin drool of blood oozed down his chin.

She held his head up so the whole group could see, and then yelled, "We can make it to San Francisco by tonight if we keep up the pace. So, let's move!"

The zombie chain gang answered with a series of grunts and moans... Mira pulled on Gwen's wrists, and the zombie's white eyes widened. But then she took a step to follow Mira's lead, and slowly the chain of dead behind her fell into line and began to instinctually follow the scent of fresh flesh from Mira who stayed ahead of them all.

The car began inching forward. And soon it began moving at almost a regular pace.

Mira grinned. She was going to finish this race after all.

XII

Deathpower

《《—》》

*A*nnouncer Karen: *You are not going to believe this, but the car of Team Beauty and the Brains is literally marching towards the finish line in San Francisco... powered by zombies!*

Announcer Bill: *I don't think we've ever seen a racer as ingenious as Beauty. She has survived the death of her driver, taken out two teams who tried to kill her, and now has zombies pulling her Mustang down the road since she ran out of fuel.*

Announcer Karen: *She has truly turned out to be the star of this race.*

Announcer Bill: *But the question remains... will she finish? Or finish in time?*

Announcer Karen: *Team Pussy Crush and Poison Pete held the lead for days now, but now have slipped to third place with 237 points. Snakegirl and Siouxsie narrowly have edged them out with 251 points. But in a flurry of kills that I am sure will be played again and again in the coming days, Beauty vaulted herself into first place with 269 points as she fended off a gang on the San Rafael bridge.*

Announcer Bill: *And those totals aren't counting the zombies that these drivers are bringing back alive with them. Nobody is going to come close to beating Beauty on that score.*

The Mustang was moving along, but Beauty knew that it wasn't going fast enough. At this rate, it would be another day before they'd reach the finish line. And even with all of her kills and captures, she could not afford to be the last one in. It was a race, and the finish position was an important chunk of the score.

She felt bad for Gwen; the zombie's skin hung in tatters from her back thanks to Tony basically cooking her on the car's hood. And Mira had ultimately forced the woman to cradle the infant in her arms (with some help from a t-shirt and rope) because the thing couldn't walk fast enough to keep up. Gwen's eyes may have been glazed over but Mira could still read her gaze. It haunted her.

It had taken forever to wind around San Quentin and finally reach the 101. She needed more power.

They were passing an old Chevy when she saw the motion inside.

Like so many that she'd seen on this trip, the driver had apparently died in the car and couldn't figure out how to get out. Beauty could fix that. She opened the door and backpeddled quickly when the creature staggered out. It followed her to the front of the zombie chain gang and when they were far enough ahead of the rest of the dead, she leveled a kick right at the thing's yellowed jaw.

The zombie teetered backward and crumpled to the ground. Set and match.

Mira didn't waste a moment. She jumped on its back, holding it down, and slipped a line of twine around the belt that still held the thing's jeans up. Then she jumped off and stood by as the creature rolled back and forth, struggling to rise again. When it was back on its feet, Mira darted to the car and added the end of the rope to the collection of ropes currently pulling on the heavy classic silver chrome bumper. Before the dead slowed too much, she ran back ahead of them. As soon as they saw—or smelled—her again, the car surged forward once more.

Mira nodded. They seemed to be moving a little faster already. She'd just needed more fuel.

She ran ahead, looking in other cars that littered the highway. She didn't see any other trapped creatures but it wasn't long before she saw a small group of the dead wandering the road a little ways ahead. You could tell the moment that they saw her; immediately their aimless shambling turned to a targeted march. It looked to be a family; a thickset man in dirty jeans and a bloodstained blue and white-checked shirt led the surge, while behind him a thin brunette in a skirt and ripped blouse clacked her jaw together in anticipation. These zombies were hungry. And their son—a high school age victim by the looks of his Nirvana t-shirt and height—literally put his arms up and pointed them in her direction.

Hungry or not, Mira didn't anticipate a problem taking them out.

And she was right.

Three kicks and the father went down. She aimed another at the teen's eager arms and cringed slightly when she heard the snap of bone as he fell.

Mira didn't even drop the woman. She darted around her with the rope, readied a knot at a safe distance, and then cinched it close. She tied one end quickly around the window frame of a nearby pickup truck, and then returned to push the teen back on the ground. The arm lay at an awkward angle, with a dangerous looking shard of bone sticking out of the skin halfway to the wrist. It was weird how it really didn't bleed. The kid was shrieking in a pretty horrible way, but that just gave Mira the time she needed to cinch the rope around his middle and drag him away from his father, now staggering towards her with a blaze of fury and hunger in his dark brown, but strangely murky eyes.

The Mustang was closing in on them and she needed to take care of this one before the chain gang reached her. Mira ran around him, confusing the zombie's attack, before she punched a foot into his back.

He went down, and she leapt onto him and pulled out the twine to fasten him... and realized then that she didn't have enough to fasten him to the car.

What the hell was she going to do with no more rope?

Shaking her head in frustration, she tied his wrists together and then leapt free before he could pin her with his legs and weight.

Mira ran to the nearby pickup, avoiding the outstretched arms of the zombie wife. She hopped into the rusty bed of the thing and looked for something, anything she could use.

A moment later, she smiled.

There were a half dozen black rubber tie cords hooked to holes in the truck. They wound around a couple of toolboxes and a ladder, to keep things from moving. Nothing had moved in that pickup truck for years.

She unfastened them all and ran back to the growling father. With a couple more dodges and feints, she was able to get the thing hooked around his belt.

Five minutes later, there were three more zombies pulling Deathasus.

Deathpower indeed.

Over the next three hours, Mira added more zombies to her chaingang. It was getting harder and harder to fasten them onto something without getting savaged by the group. But she didn't need any more now. The car was moving along fast, almost too fast, as the mob of hungry, angry zombies struggled to walk faster to catch the warm-blooded girl just a few feet in front of them.

Mira found herself struggling to move fast enough to stay ahead of the car. She was exhausted. She had never gone through so much in one week. She had never fought so much in one day. Her entire body was streaked with sweat and caked with blood. It was no wonder the zombies were struggling harder to get to her. She felt ripe as a compost pile.

But it was finally almost over.

As the zombies dragged the Mustang onto the Golden Gate Bridge, Mira almost cried with relief. They wound around the few cars that remained abandoned on the bridge and soon, she could see the gateway to San Francisco. A throng of people waited beyond that well-barricaded entry point. She could see heads and arms waving excitedly all along the spectator deck at the top. In just a few more minutes, the doors would open temporarily to let her in.

Mira looked at the road behind her, and saw a cloud of dust in the distance along the winding road she'd just left. One of the other two remaining San Francisco drivers. Maybe Macklin Mortis. She didn't have much time before the other car got here. It was time to make her entrance.

She ran around the mob of marching zombies quickly and reached in through the moving Mustang's open window to the driver's seat. Her hand came back wrapped in greasy black hair. Flies fled in a cloud from the gaping mouth.

"Let's move!" she cried, running back to the front of the line. She held up the bloody, severed head of Tony once more—their gruesome totem—and began to run towards the finish with it swinging from her outstretched arm. She looked like a savage, leading a massacre charge.

The zombies responded to her energy, surging forward faster than ever as the giant metal doors ahead creaked slowly open to allow Deathasus to roll inside. They couldn't resist the scent of a very deadly Beauty leading them to the finish line... holding all that remained of Brains.

XIII

Feral Finish

《《—》》

Announcer Karen: Unbelievable! Beauty has crossed the finish line in San Francisco, just behind Snake Girl and Siouxsie, who arrived at their finish in New York five minutes ago. Macklin Mortis entered the San Francisco gates right behind her, but all eyes were on Beauty and the grisly remains of her partner and her ghastly undead team. Beauty has outscored them all on kills and live zombies, Bill. The judges are discussing the final tally now, but I don't think there's any question about the winner.

Announcer Bill: Nobody has ever brought back 17 walking zombies before. Beauty has set a new record.

Announcer Karen: She's also set the stands in chaos. The zombies are straining to get loose from the ropes of her car to get at the hundreds of people running away from the finish line. The car has stopped moving completely now, as the dead are throwing themselves in different directions at the closest spectators.

Announcer Bill: The race reclamation crew is working to stun and remove the zombies from their ropes one by one, to add them to the cages below the stands. They may be alarming to the fans now, but they'll be put into service on treadmills to generate power for the city. With all of these undead, Beauty has definitely upped the wattage in San Francisco today!

Announcer Karen: Wait. What is she doing now? She's going to get herself killed right after winning the race!

Announcer Bill: She appears to be talking to one of the zombies! This may count against her score if she lets this thing get free, not that it probably would matter at this point...

Mira held the head of Brains up to the crowd as she staggered across the finish line. The response from the crowd in the stands all around her was deafening. And then she threw the head down on the pavement in a gesture of both victory and repulsion and wiped the slimy residue of the asshole off her hands and onto her shorts as it rolled away. She was finally through with Tony, at last.

The race officials were already removing the zombies from her car before the things could get free and kill any of the fans, but there were some close calls as her chain gang swung rotting arms and lunged with manic, hungry teeth at their new captors.

One of the officials delicately pried the zombie toddler from Gwen's arms, as another began to move in to grab Gwen's rope. But from the lost look in Gwen's milky eyes, Mira didn't think the official had to worry. The zombie looked utterly beaten.

"Step back from her a minute," Mira asked. She'd been thinking a lot about Gwen over the past few hours. How they'd picked her up, and how she'd been used.

The race official looked confused, but after hesitating a moment, did as she asked.

Mira held up one finger. "Wait until I come back." She ran behind the car and popped the trunk. Then she reached in and pulled out Tony's favorite toy.

Mira took it to the front of the Mustang where the race official still waited, guarding Gwen, a shock rod ready in his hand. She stepped in front of him and made eye contact with the zombie.

"I'm sorry about all this," she said. "I have no problem killing zombies. You *should* be dead. Like, *not moving* dead. But what Tony did to you was shit. I have to admit, it was comforting hearing you in the backseat these past couple days. I needed the company. And now I just can't let them give you any more misery than you've already had."

Gwen made a strange sound in her yellowed throat. It might have been a sob. Or relief.

Mira took it as a thank you, and with a faint, sad smile, brought the machete around fast. She gave Tony credit for one thing in that moment. The machete's blade was razor sharp.

The zombie's head bounced and rolled across the ground, a spatter of black blood staining Mira's yellow shoes. And then Gwen's face lay quiet at last, staring sightless at the bright blue sky. Mira dropped the blade with a clatter right next to it and began to walk away.

"She won't bite you now," she told the race official as she passed. He looked stunned, unsure what to do.

Mira stopped and closed her eyes for a second, letting the lurid events of the past few days stream through her mind once more. It had all been so... ridiculous. Then she took a deep breath, accepting the insanity, and slowly began to walk towards the winner's circle to claim her prize.

Afterword

«« — »»

Living Death Race has one of the longest, strangest gestations of any story I've ever written. It all began 14 years ago, in late 2010, when James Roy Daley, publisher of Books of the Dead Press, approached me about being part of a multi-author zombie-spin book riffing off the cult film *Death Race 2000*. The idea was that six authors would write stories following race teams competing in an apocalyptic Mad Max kind of road story, where all were in a cross-country race with the goal being to kill as many zombies as possible. A seventh author would serve as the race "announcer" and essentially stitch the various stories together as all the racers struggled to reach the finish. Two of the teams were predetermined to die before the finish... of the remaining four teams, the narrator would determine the winner.

I love *Death Race 2000*, and it was a really fun concept, so I signed on immediately. But the project was plagued from the start. Roy had a couple authors agree but then drop out early on, and he had to look for replacements. With his confirmation in early 2011 that the project was still a go, I dove in and wrote a 15,000-word story for it called "Beauty and the Brains." I was the first one to the writing finish line in June 2011, and Roy and I joked about whether that meant my team got to win. Weston Ochse and Matt Hults also turned in segments.

But then the project stalled. More authors dropped out.

Four years later, in 2015, Roy tried to resuscitate the book with just the three of us who had turned in team stories. He was going to write the narrator part himself to tie our stories together into a unified whole. A few months later, in the summer of 2016, Roy sent around edits to our stories. There was a short flurry of email activity as we talked about potentially releasing the book to coincide with the *Death Race 2050* movie coming in January 2017.

But then things got quiet again.

Like many of the publishing houses that got rich quick from the early boom of e-books, Roy's publishing company had gone from being a full-time job to a struggling, part-time press. Finally, in November 2017, over six years after I turned in my draft story, he officially pulled the plug on the book once and for all.

By that point, my story had "sat in the drawer" so long, that I didn't really care. I was busy working on novels, and idly thought that maybe at some point, I'd brush the story off and try to find it a home. But it was too long for magazines, and too short for a novella.

Living Death Race consequently sat in the drawer for over six more years.

And then, early in 2024, I came across the story file on my hard drive again and reread it for the first time in ages. And you know what?

I really liked it.

Mira is a super badass fun character, and the story still felt fresh and fun to me. It was almost like reading a piece from someone else, since I hadn't revisited it in so long. I'd forgotten most of it.

I decided that when I was done with my edits for my next novel, I'd take a shot (finally) at retooling it a little, making sure it really could stand alone without the other pieces it was originally supposed to be paired with and find it a home at long last.

Once I started editing, I got more excited about the project and I reached out to K. Trap Jones to see if it was something The Evil Cookie Publishing would be interested in taking a look at it. He was... and then I really dug in earnest to finish it. I decided that adding a couple of chapters showing Beauty and the Brains meeting the other teams in the race would broaden the scope and complete the story more. I also implemented the original idea of having a narrator voice talk about the race to provide more context. By the time I'd finished adding those elements and fleshing out some things in the original chapters, I'd nearly doubled the length of the story, and Gwen, in particular, gained some more screen time. Now it is a full novella, while maintaining and expanding on all of the things I loved about the original story.

I hope you had as good of a time on the road with Mira and Tony and Gwen as I did.

While the original project didn't pan out, I have to thank James Roy Daley for coming up with the concept and pulling me into a driver's seat for this Living Death Race. And I have to thank K. Trap Jones for helping me to finally see the journey through to the finish.

I was right there with Mira at the end when she threw that bloody head down on the asphalt in victory.

At last.

The Death Race is run!

John Everson

June 2024
Naperville, IL

About the Author

《《 — 》》

John Everson is a staunch advocate for the culinary joys of the jalapeño and an unabashed fan of 1970s European horror cinema. He is also the Bram Stoker Award-winning author of *Covenant* and its sequels *Sacrifice* and *Redemption*, as well as a dozen other novels, including the erotic horror tour de force and Bram Stoker Award finalist *NightWhere*, the haunting thriller *Voodoo Heart* and his latest giallo homage, *The Bloodstained Doll*. Other novels include *Five Deaths for Seven Songbirds, The Pumpkin Man, Siren, The 13th* and the spider-driven *Violet Eyes*.

Over the past 30 years, his short fiction has appeared in more than 75 magazines and anthologies and received a number of critical accolades, including frequent Honorable Mentions in the *Year's Best Fantasy & Horror* anthology series. His story "Letting Go" was a Bram Stoker Award finalist in 2007 and "The Pumpkin Man" was included in the anthology *All American Horror: The Best of the First Decade of the 21st Century*. He has written licensed tie-in stories for *The Green Hornet* and *Kolchak The Night Stalker* and novelettes for *The Vampire Diaries* and Jonathan Maberry's *V-Wars* universe (Books 1 and 3). *V-Wars* was turned into a 10-episode NetFlix series in 2019 that included two of Everson's characters, Danika and Mila Dubov.

His short story collections include *Cage of Bones & Other Deadly Obsessions, Needles & Sins, Vigilantes of Love* and *Sacrificing Virgins*. To catch up on his blog, join his newsletter or get information on his fiction, art and music, visit www.johneverson.com.

@TheEvilCookiePublishing

Subscribe to The Evil Cookie Publishing YouTube Channel to watch cover artwork videos and see the creative behind-the-scenes of your favorite books.

FOLLOW FOR UPDATES

Facebook: theevilcookiepublishing
Instagram: theevilcookiepublishing
X: @EvilCookiePub

WEBSITE

www.theevilcookie.com

Made in the USA
Columbia, SC
10 September 2024

41486231R00063